CW01624511

FIN
THE LADY

An enthralling crime mystery full of twists

ROGER SILVERWOOD

Yorkshire Murder Mysteries Book 10

JOFFE BOOKS

Revised edition 2020
Joffe Books, London
www.joffebooks.com

First published 2008

This book is a work of fiction. Names, characters, businesses, organisations, places and events are either the product of the author's imagination or are used fictitiously. Any resemblance to actual persons, living or dead, events or locales is entirely coincidental. The spelling used is British English except where fidelity to the author's rendering of accent or dialect supersedes this. The right of Roger Silverwood to be identified as author of this work has been asserted by him in accordance with the Copyright, Designs and Patents Act 1988.

© Roger Silverwood

ISBN: 978-1-78931-338-3

CHAPTER ONE

London, U.K. Monday, 1 January 2007

A man was found shot dead in his first-floor flat, on Upper Sackville Street in the West End of London. He had been shot at point-blank range with clinical precision: one bullet .202 calibre straight through the forehead. There had been no report from the neighbourhood of a gunshot, so it was assumed that the pistol had been fitted with a silencer. On the body of the dead man, the murderer left a small white card with black printing, like a visiting card, that simply read: 'With the compliments of Reynard.' Also, pieces of orange peel were found at the scene of the crime, from which it was assumed that Reynard ate an orange after he had committed the murder.

That New Year's Day murder was the twenty-second killing by Reynard using the same MO. The police had made no progress in identifying and apprehending the murderer. He was assumed to be a man, who worked alone. Many of the murders had been committed in London, but there had also been cases in other parts of the country and as far north as Newcastle-on-Tyne. In seven years, he had murdered more than eighteen men and four women that the police knew about. The motive for each murder was not known, although it was invariably established after their deaths that the victims had had criminal records or had been suspected of criminal activities.

The newspapers were having a field day. Whenever Reynard struck, the press, particularly the tabloids, filled their pages with every detail of the new crime and compared it with the earlier ones attributed to him, and gleefully published cartoons and disdainful copy, ridiculing the police force for their inability to bring Reynard to book.

Even in these sophisticated days of DNA, it seemed that there had never been any kind of substance, human fluid, matter or hair left behind at the scene, or anywhere else, that could be attributed to him. Every policeman in the UK was desperate to unmask and arrest him. Profilers at all levels had been making projections, but with such limited information their reports had not proved adequate.

Each of the forty-three forces, as well as the Serious Organised Crime Agency (SOCA) newly formed on 3 April 2006, was put on special watch for master serial murderer, Reynard.

WAKEFIELD, WEST YORKSHIRE, U.K. 0400 HOURS. MONDAY, 8 JANUARY, 2007

The sky was as black as an undertaker's cat.

The heavy steel gates at Wakefield Prison, a category A secure unit, rattled open and a Group 4 white van with two uniformed men in the cab, nosed its way out. It turned left onto Love Lane and made its way through quiet, deserted halogen-lit streets and shadowy shuttered shops towards the A642 and from there onto the M1.

The white van held two crooks, each locked in separately in the small, sweaty cages in the back. One of the crooks was Eddie 'The Cat' Glazer, a ruthless career bank robber and murderer, as hard-boiled as a ten-minute egg. He was serving thirty years for the manslaughter of a security guard in

Sheffield in 2001. The other was Harry Harrison, a jewellery thief and confidence trickster: one of several thousand ... too stupid to be honest ... even more stupid to get caught.

The British penal system provided for the timely movement of prisoners from time to time, so that they did not get too knowledgeable about routines and develop such relationships with prison officers or others that they might begin to devise ways of escape.

Time hangs heavy in the cells. It's the only commodity of which there's an oversupply and prisoners have to do something with their grey matter when cooped up behind bars twenty-four seven. Some spend their time conjuring up schemes to acquire more drugs and money, others fantasize on how to get more women and enjoy better sex, but most all of them dream how to escape from the ungodly place.

There was hardly any traffic on the damp city roads that January morning at that unsociable hour. A lone taxi and an articulated ASDA lorry circled a roundabout as the powerful Group 4 van's headlights picked its way out of the city and eventually joined the A642. The road twisted and turned, but progress was rapid. The van had travelled only two miles out of the city however, when, coming up to a bridge over a railway line, where the road narrowed, the van's headlights suddenly picked out two cars in the middle of the road; they appeared to have been in a serious collision. They blocked the road so that it was impossible for the van to continue its journey. The headlights of both damaged cars shone brightly but futilely; white steam issued from under a mangled bonnet and black smoke still puffed out from one of the car's exhaust pipes.

The security driver slowed and the van headlights picked out a man lying flat on the wet road by the open door of one car. Part of his head was in a dreadful state, covered with a red glutinous liquid. A woman in the driving seat of the other car was slumped awkwardly over the driving wheel, her hair sticking out in every direction.

The Group 4 drivers had a strict protocol to deal with situations of this sort. After all, this could be a mock event staged in an attempt to release their prisoners. They promptly checked that their cab doors were locked and immediately radioed the nearest police station, which was Wakefield Westgate, and informed them of the RTA and their situation. The duty police sergeant reminded them to treat the incident with suspicion and caution, and advised that an ambulance and police support would be despatched instantly and that their ETA would be 12 minutes.

The Group 4 men eyed the scene with concern. They saw the man on the road move slightly as if having now regained limited consciousness. They could hear him calling for help. They drove the van closer until the light beam shone directly onto him. He appeared to be in great pain and as he turned to face the van they could see his face was a gory mess. He was moving his head slightly from side to side, as if he wanted to say something, and then they heard a cry from the woman in the other car.

It was too much for the driver and his mate to ignore. They decided to venture out and see if they could assist them. They opened the cab doors and the next thing they knew they were flying through the air like pilots in ejector seats. They had been pulled out by a couple of huge men in balaclavas, jeans and trainers. When the policemen picked themselves up from the road, they were looking down the barrels of old Sten guns.

The two pretending to be injured, wiped the banana and tomato ketchup off their faces, pulled on balaclavas and dashed round to support the gunmen.

No words were used. Prods with the shotguns soon had the Group 4 men at the side door of the van, unlocking it. They pushed up the step. One of the heavies peered through a narrow slot into one of the cages.

Glazer peered back. He was holding onto the door and jumping up and down, his face was red, his eyes darting round in all directions.

'Come on, Tony,' Glazer screamed. 'Hurry up! Come on!'

The key was turned, the door opened and he shot out as though he was at the end of a piece of elastic.

The woman leaped forward and wrapped her arms round his neck.

'You're out, Eddie. You're out!' she squealed.

She kissed him hard on the lips but he pushed her away.

'Yeah. Yeah. Let's get away from here.'

There was a loud knocking from the next cage.

The heavies rammed the two Group 4 men into Glazer's compartment: it was a tight squeeze. They closed the door and turned the key.

There was more knocking and some yelling from the next cage. A voice screamed, 'Let me out. Don't leave me here!'

It was Harry Harrison.

Tony Glazer looked at his brother who said, 'Let's go. Leave the bastard there.'

The Glazers, Oona and the two heavies stepped down from the van.

Harry Harrison yelled through the peephole in the door.

'I've got money, Mr Glazer. Honest. Ten thousand pounds stashed away. You can have it all.'

Eddie Glazer turned back and said, 'Where?'

'In Wakefield. Just let me out of here. You can have it all.'

Oona yelled, 'Come on, Eddie. The cops'll could be here anytime.'

'You'd better not be kidding me. When can you get it?'

'This afternoon. Come on, Mr Glazer. I never done you no harm, have I? We're mates, aren't we?'

'You'd better be on the level,' Eddie Glazer yelled.

Glazer turned to the heavy with the keys.

'Right,' he said with a nod. 'Let him out, Ox.'

The door opened and out shot Harry Harrison. He closed it quickly and gave a big sigh.

'Come on,' yelled Tony Glazer to his brother.

'You're coming with us,' Eddie said to Harrison grabbing him by the neck of his coat.

Tony Glazer's eyes flashed. 'We've no bloody room!'

'He's worth ten grand to me. *Find* room!'

The gang left the van, its external side door open, swinging in the night air. They dashed down the banking to the rail track. A minute later, Eddie 'The Cat' Glazer was in a sidecar attached to a Honda 500 being driven alongside the railway track by his younger brother, Tony. Eddie's wife, Oona, had her arms tight round his waist. Close behind them was another Honda motorbike with the two heavies and little Harry Harrison sitting precariously on the mudguard.

The two motorbikes noisily sprayed out silver grey gravel as they sped away into the night.

BROMERSLEY, SOUTH YORKSHIRE, U.K. 1800 HOURS. MONDAY, 5 FEBRUARY 2007

Simon Spencer looked round at the gloomy pub wallpaper, the scratched woodwork, the smeared dull copper work and the dusty tables strewn with empty bottles and dirty glasses.

'Light ale,' the bartender said, banging the bottle down in front of him. 'That's two pounds. Haven't seen you in here before, John,' he said pointedly with a sniff.

Spencer looked round at the quiet crowd of twenty-five or so drinkers; some were smoking cigarettes, standing around snatching teatime anaesthetic to bolster them up before going home to their nagging wives and irritating children for a boring evening watching repeats in front of the television, or mooching round houses, shops, offices, garages and warehouses looking for an unlocked door or an undemanding window to gain easy access, where, in the secret of the night, they might find something transportable and easy to sell.

Spencer glanced from man to man. As he did so, each in turn averted his eyes and sought cover by supping from a glass, taking the opportunity to turn away dragging even harder on his cigarette.

At length Spencer turned to the big tattooed man with the little gold ring in his ear and said, 'I'm looking for somebody.'

'No somebodies in here, John. All nobodies,' the bartender said as he took the coins and tossed them into the open till drawer. He wiped the top of the counter with a dirty bar towel. His eyes narrowed. 'What sort of somebody?' he asked after a pause. 'Has the body got a name?'

Spencer took his time. Spoke slowly, carefully choosing his words. He looked across the bar room, then nonchalantly said: 'Oh, somebody … anybody, who wants to earn a few hundred quid. Easy like.'

The bartender blinked.

'A few hundred?'

Spencer shrugged and picked up the bottle.

'Everybody's up for that, John, I reckon,' the bartender added.

Spencer took another gulp of the beer.

'It's a special kind of man. A man who maybe wouldn't mind … maybe … bending the rules a bit.'

The barman looked at him closely then shook his head thoughtfully.

'There'd be nobody here interested in anything dishonest, John,' he said warily.

'Not dishonest,' Spencer protested irritably. 'Just a wee bit … out of the ordinary, that's all. And why do you keep calling me John?'

'I call everybody John, John.'

A man came up to the bar. The barman turned away to serve him.

Spencer shrugged and slowly finished the beer. He looked round at the other drinkers in the little bar. They deliberately turned away from him when they felt the possibility that a glance from him might change into a hard intrusive look. He slowly finished his drink. He wrinkled his nose. He was disappointed with his foray into Bromersley's unfriendly grubby backwater alehouse. He pulled up his coat collar and strode out of The Fisherman's Rest on Canal Street. This thoroughfare was a short, unmade road that ran parallel to Bromersley canal for a few hundred yards before it joined the main road. The canal was a smelly, slow-flowing stretch of water from which, he had heard, dead bodies had been fished by the local constabulary from time to time.

Spencer hardly gave the water a glance. His mind was on other things as he trudged his way along the path to the main road on his way to the bus station.

He passed ten terraced houses whose front doors abutted the pavement. There were ginnels at every second house to give access to the back doors. As he passed the last ginnel, he suddenly heard a scuffling sound and then a man's soft whisper.

'Hey, copper. What you doing slumming round here?'

Spencer turned and in the moonlight, saw a man in a suit, shirt and collar. In the crisp February moonlight he could see that he was holding something shiny and black in his hand and pointing it at him.

He didn't like what he saw.

He put his hands up … because … he had seen old films in the old cinema picture show and he thought it was the sensible thing to do.

'Who are you?' Spencer said. 'And what do you want?'

'I ashed you first, brudder. I tell you, we don't like plain-clothes coppers creeping round our places. And you're sure getting brave coming round here in ones.'

'I'm not a policeman. And I can prove it, but who are you?'

The man waved the gun boldly. He didn't believe him.

'Oh yes? This ain't no lollipop I'm holding in my hand, brudder. It sort of gives me an advantage, don't you think?'

Spencer swallowed.

'Look, friend, I've got a wallet in my inside pocket. It's got more than a hundred pounds in it. Take it, why don't you?'

The man with the gun blinked.

Spencer stuck his chest forward and slightly inclined his body towards him.

The man hesitated. He licked his lips and said: 'Keep still then. No tricks.' He reached out. His hot, sticky fingers touched Spencer's coat lapel, dipped swiftly into the inside pocket and professionally, between first and second fingers, lifted out the fat leather wallet.

It was quick and smooth. Spencer didn't feel a thing.

The gunman tried to open the wallet.

Spencer took a step towards him.

He saw him. 'Stay where you are,' he said nervously and backed away. He tugged harder at the wallet. It was reluctant to open. He tugged at it harder. Then suddenly, he managed it. That quick positive action triggered the cunningly set up ignition of a strip of magnesium, by dragging an ordinary match quickly past two pieces of sandpaper held tight with an elastic band. The result was a blinding white light lasting for about a second.

The dazzle was long enough.

The gunman yelled and instinctively dropped the wallet.

Spencer reached out for the man's wrist, gave it a sharp twist and then held onto it. The gunman was on the floor and the gun rattled across the pavement into the gutter. Spencer kicked him under the chin, let go of his arm and picked up the gun. Then he reached down over the stunned man and recovered the wallet. The gunman groaned and rubbed his jaw.

'You shouldn't be pulling guns on strangers,' Spencer said with a grin. 'You could get yourself killed. Stand up,' he added waving the gun in his direction.

The man got to his feet still rubbing his jaw.

'That *hurt*, copper,' he groaned. 'You know, I could *do* you for assault.'

'And if I was a policeman, I could arrest you for assault with a deadly weapon.'

'Don't get too cocky, old chum. That ain't a pukkha gun you're waving about there, and it ain't loaded. And if you ain't a copper, what do you want mooching round hereabouts?'

'I ain't – I'm not a policeman.'

He took a step back from the man and fumbled for the safety catch. It couldn't be moved. It wasn't movable. He depressed a catch and the cartridge holder came free; it weighed very little. It was made of plastic. He snorted and threw the replica at him.

'Catch.'

He caught it and put it in his pocket.

'And if I couldn't get you for assault with a deadly weapon,' Spencer continued, 'I'd look at your record and find something else I could book you for.'

'If you're not a copper, you couldn't get to see my record.'

'Maybe I could bribe a policeman to let me have a copy of it.'

The young man stopped and looked at Spencer thoughtfully.

'If you're not a copper, you must be a private investigator.'

'No.'

Mystified, he said: 'Here. What do you really want, then?'

'Somebody who wants to earn a few hundred quid. Easy like.'

'A few hundred?'

Spencer shrugged.

'Maybe a few thousand.'

'I might be interested.'

'I need a special kind of man. A man who maybe wouldn't mind bending the rules a bit.'

He grinned.

'Might be able to do that.'

'Somebody reliable. Somebody bold. Somebody who could pretend to be somebody he isn't.'

'What's the catch, brudder?'

'There's no catch. You just have to do exactly what I tell you.'

CHAPTER TWO

Creesforth Road, Bromersley, South Yorkshire, U.K.
1400 hours. Monday, 16 July 2007.

The taxi pulled up at a leafy, detached house on the expensive side of the town. The sun was shining. The sky was blue and cloudless and yet the birds weren't singing; in fact, there was an eerie quiet, as if time was suspended.

A chubby woman in a sundress, relaxing on a canvas chair, could be observed in her garden through the cupressus, applying cream to her arms and shoulders.

'Number twenty-two, ma'am,' the taxi driver said to his fare in the back. 'That's what you said, isn't it, ma'am?' he said.

A figure in light blue, with a big straw hat affording shelter from the sun, and wearing Ashanti mirrored sunglasses answered him.

'Twenty-two, the Beeches. Exactly so, my man. Is the fare the same as before?' the high-pitched delicate voice enquired.

The taxi driver had no idea what the customer might have paid before. 'It's six pounds, missis,' he said irritably. 'It's allus six pounds from Wells Street Baths to Creesforth

Road. You gotta cross town and it allus takes a lot of time, you know.'

There was a click from the fastening of a handbag.

'Oh yes. I understand. That's quite all right.'

The big long hand in the white glove shot over his shoulder waving a ten pound note.

'Keep the change, my man.'

The driver's face brightened.

'Oh thank you, ma'am,' he said, swiftly thrusting the note into his trouser pocket with a big smile. 'Now, do you want a hand with your bag?'

The nearside door of the taxi opened and out came a long nylon-covered leg. 'No thank you. Now, what's your name?'

'Bert Amersham, ma'am.'

'Well now, Mr Amersham—'

'Call me Bert, ma'am. I answers well enough to Bert.'

'Well, Bert. I am Lady Cora Blessington. The time is exactly two o'clock. Now, you will collect me at three o'clock exactly, won't you?'

The taxi driver looked with more interest at the fare since he had received the handsome tip. She was not a handsome woman. Rather gawky, he thought, and the fluffy old-fashioned blue dress would have been more suited to a much younger woman.

'I'll be here on the button, ma'am. You can depend on it.'

A man in a suit, white shirt and tie came through the front gate of the house next door. He saw the figure in powder blue pushing open the gate of Number 22. He looked the summery apparition up and down, smiled self-consciously and said, 'Good afternoon.'

'Good afternoon,' the figure in blue replied with a coy smile and made a way up the path.

The sunbather from next door waved across the fence.

'Beautiful weather, Lady Cora,' she called. 'Wonderful afternoon.'

'Fabulous,' came the reply in the high-pitched delicate voice, and with a royal wave added, 'We must enjoy it while we can.'

It was sound advice.

Someone was about to be murdered.

Detective Inspector Angel's Office, Bromersley Police Station, South Yorkshire U.K. 1400 hours. Monday, 16 July 2007.

There was a knock at the door.

'Come in,' Angel called.

A young probationer policeman, Ahmed Ahaz entered. He pulled open the door, held the knob and, like a flunky at a palace, made the announcement. 'Miss Smith, sir.'

A pretty young woman came in. Angel smiled, quickly stood up and pointed at the chair next to his desk.

'Please sit down, Miss Smith.'

He nodded at PC Ahaz who went out and closed the door.

The young woman looked round the little dowdy green-painted office, and quickly took stock: a cleared desk top with a pile of post in the centre of it; a swivel chair; a filing cabinet; stationery cupboard; a small table; a telephone and two ordinary wooden chairs. By the look on her face, she had perhaps expected more impressive surroundings for the celebrated police inspector.

She sat down, put her small handbag on her knees and gave a little cough.

Angel looked up from the desk and straight into her eyes.

'Now then, you wanted to see me, Miss Smith?'

'Yes. I asked to see you, Inspector Angel. I had read so much about you in the newspapers, I felt as if … as if, I knew you … ever so slightly. I mean I don't know *any* policemen at all really. Never had reason even to call in at a police station. So I thought I would ask to see you by name. I hope that's all right. You see, I am very worried.'

'Of course. Of course. You want to report a crime?'

Her face straightened.

'Yes. Indeed I do,' she said positively.

He nodded.

'It's like this,' she began then stopped.

Angel peered at her and said: 'Please continue. In your own time.'

'It's rather tedious, I am afraid. I don't know quite where to start.'

'Start wherever you want to.'

'I'll try to tell you in sequence, Inspector.'

He nodded encouragingly.

'Well, my father was the proprietor of Smith's Glassworks. He was a widower, and when he died ten years ago, he left the business to my brother John and me. I was not the slightest bit interested in it. The business made fancy shaped bottles. Short batch runs for perfume companies and customers of that sort. I left the day-to-day running of the business entirely to my brother. I had a little capital of my own and I run a riding stables up in Tunistone. That keeps me busy enough. I received dividends on a quarterly basis from the business and that's all I cared about glass bottles. Now, just about two years ago, my brother rang me up and said he had had an offer for the company from an American conglomerate and he asked me my feelings about selling up. I said I didn't care much one way or the other. He told me how much was involved. It sounded most attractive so we agreed to sell to them. A few weeks later, the deal was completed and, after paying off all the creditors, the bank loan and the capital gains tax, we expected to net almost two million pounds. I would have received half of that. John said that he would put the cheque from the American company safely on deposit as the following day he was taking his wife and my two nieces on holiday to the island of Phuket for Christmas to celebrate the deal. I saw them off at the station, and, tragically, that was the last I saw of them.'

Angel pursed his lips as he began to anticipate what was coming next.

'You will recall the tsunami on that horrific Boxing Day, 2004.'

He certainly did. Who could forget the pictures? He nodded sympathetically.

'Eventually, the Home Office notified me officially that they had all been killed.'

'Dreadful,' Angel said. 'Losing an entire family like that.'

She nodded and wiped away a tear.

'And what can I do to help?' He said gently.

'Well,' she sighed. 'The money has apparently disappeared.'

Angel blinked, then frowned.

'Where did your brother bank the cheque?'

'There's the rub,' she said. 'He didn't tell me and I didn't think to ask. He said it was banked at a good interest and that he would settle the tax with the revenue and then make the final distribution on his return. That was all right by me, at the time. I was in no hurry. However, time has gone on. John didn't return. Naturally, I thought a statement from the bank or building society or wherever it had been invested would have been sent out by now ... obviously to his last known address. As his next of kin, I have dealt with his affairs, cleared his house and indeed, sold it. But no sign of the investment has shown up, either among his papers or by post. Now the Inland Revenue are chasing me for the tax on the sale, which is a mighty sum.'

Angel screwed up his face in sympathy and eyed her carefully.

'Your brother definitely received the cheque?'

'Definitely. He phoned me. He couldn't contain himself; he *had* to boast. It was a certified cheque, he said, for two million pounds.'

'But you have no idea what he did with it?'

'That's the problem.'

'He didn't deposit it where his personal account is?'

'No. We discussed that. The interest rate for a large sum on short term deposit wasn't competitive. But I have no idea where he placed it.'

'Hmm. You could start with the Americans.'

'They can only confirm it was cashed through the currency exchange in a lump sum and then paid out in sterling with thousands of other payments, which means it's impossible to trace.'

Angel sighed. He rubbed his chin. The cogs began to go round. His first thought was to say that it was a civil case, but, then, as he thought about it, he realized a crime had definitely been committed. Every investment house worth its salt would want to find the depositor if a deposit had been left in its hands for a much longer time than had been originally arranged. Somebody must know something about it. This was a case for the fraud squad, but he knew they were up to their eyes in a particularly big foreign bank case that was also monopolizing the media's interest.

It wasn't feasible to attempt to search every single deposit account in every bank, building society, insurance company and investment house in every currency in the UK over the past two years. He would need warrants and security passes and it would take forever. There must be something he could do. He needed time. Time to think about it and decide what to do.

'Well, I'll need the date your brother received the cheque.'

'That's easy. It was a memorable day. It was the 17th December 2004.'

'And I need your name and address and telephone number and your brother's last address in Bromersley.'

'Certainly. I'll write them down, shall I?'

The phone rang. He reached out for it.

'Angel?

It was the superintendent.

'Come up here, smartish,' he said abruptly, and replaced the receiver.

It sounded urgent. Angel wrinkled his nose. He left the report he was reading and went out of the office. He strode up the green corridor to the door marked 'Detective Superintendent Horace Harker', knocked, pressed down the handle and pushed it open.

'Come in,' Harker yelled.

'You wanted me, sir?'

There was a smell of TCP wafting round the room. Angel was used to it. Harker must have a cold again. His nose must have been running like a bath tap, as it was red around the nostrils and his mouth was turned down like the drawing of a villain in a children's cartoon strip. He reached out to the wire tray at the front of his desk, took out a small slip of paper and looked down at it.

'Aye. A treble nine. Just come in. A dead body found by a neighbour up at The Beeches, 22 Creesforth Road. Hmmm. Must be somebody with a bit of brass. Woman by the name of Prophet, Alicia Prophet. Thought to be murder.'

Angel's pulse rate increased by ten beats a minute. A murder case always brought him to life. The news made his heart pump that bit harder. Something also happened inside his head: it was like a jumbo jet on the tarmac, revving its engine before take-off. He thought that solving murders was what God had put him on this earth to do. And it may have been so; he had no hobbies and no other interests apart from his wife and their garden.

He knew of a solicitor's practice in Bromersley called, simply, 'Prophet and Sellman'. It was an unusual name; the victim had probably had something to do with that.

'Have you advised SOCO, sir?'

'Yes, and Doctor Mac.'

'And who reported it?'

'Next-door neighbour. A Mrs Duplessis.'

'Right, sir,' he said and made for the door. He charged up the corridor and barged into the CID room.

PC Ahaz was working at a computer at his desk near the door.

'Ah, there you are, Ahmed.'

The young man stopped staring at the screen and jumped to his feet.

'I want you to find Ron Gawber and Trevor Crisp.'

'Right, sir.'

'Tell them to meet me A.S.A.P. at 22 Creesforth Road? I'm going there now.'

'Right, sir.'

'There's a report that a woman's been murdered.'

Ahmed's jaw dropped an inch. He'd been on the force for four years now; he was still a probationer and was expecting to be a fully-fledged constable by Christmas next. Although he had been on DI Angel's team from his very first day at Bromersley nick, and had been involved in more than thirty cases of death from various causes, the news of a murder still had a disturbing effect on him.

Angel pulled up his BMW behind the white SOCO van on Creesford Road under the shade of a horse chestnut tree. It was a beautiful summer's day but he noticed that nobody seemed to be outside, taking advantage of the hot sun … not in their front gardens anyway. This struck Angel as unusual, if not meaningful. He opened the gate of The Beeches and made his way up the path.

The front door opened and a man in a white paper suit, hood, wellingtons and so on came out; he was carrying a large polythene bag. He saw Angel and pulled down the face mask.

It was DS Donald Taylor, in charge of SOCO on the Bromersley force.

'What've you got, Don?' Angel asked.

Taylor shook his head sadly.

'Murder, sir, almost certain. Woman. In her forties. Name of Alicia Prophet. Solicitor's wife. Wound in her head. I think it happened less than an hour ago. No disturbance. No apparent break in. Dr Mac's working on her now.'

'Right. Does she live here on her own?'

'No. Husband's a solicitor. Practice in town. Prophet and Sellman.'

'Has he been told?'

'Not by us, sir.'

Angel pulled a face. He reckoned he'd be the one having to do the telling.

'Was the door unlocked?'

'It was wide open, sir,' he said nodding at the big house next door. 'The lady next door was hovering around when we arrived. She says she knows who's done it. She was a witness. A Lady Blessington.'

Angel brightened. That would be a great start: an eyewitness, maybe. He wondered. 'Lady Blessington?' he said. 'A name to be conjured with. A member of the aristocracy? Did she say why she was here?'

'No, sir,' he said and made his way to the SOCO van.

Angel followed him down the path.

A car drove up and braked noisily. It was DS Gawber, who dashed out of the car and up to Angel, who went over to him.

'It's a murder, Ron. Only about an hour ago. Mrs Alicia Prophet. Do the door-to-door. I'm going into this one, Number 24.'

'Right, sir,' Gawber said and rushed off.

Angel unlatched the gate and rushed up the crazy-paved path through a well maintained lawn to the door. He saw the illuminated bell push and pressed it. The door opened immediately. A tubby, middle-aged woman with a red face and thick bottle-bottom spectacles greeted him. She was clearly distressed: agitated, touching her face, swallowing and licking her lips frequently.

'Mrs Duplessis?'

'Yes. Are you the police?' she croaked.

'Yes. I am DI Angel.'

Her cheeks were moist and she wiped them with a tissue. She had obviously been crying.

'Excuse me,' she said. 'I am so upset.'

'Of course. Of course,' he said gently. 'I am so sorry to press the matter, but time may be of the essence. I understand you were a witness to the—'

'Come in. Come in.'

He went in and she closed the door quickly.

'Sit down, please.'

'What happened,' Angel said quickly. 'What exactly did you see?'

'I know who the murderer must have been. It's unbelievable. No doubt about it.'

'What did you see?' he said urgently.

She shook her head, licked her lips and said: 'Lady Blessington arrived by taxi next door at about two o'clock. She must have been with dear Alicia Prophet for about an hour or less then came rushing out looking rather flustered. She didn't look across to me. She seemed too anxious to get away. She dropped her handbag on the path. It opened up and spilled out. Anyway, a taxi rolled up. She got into it and rushed off. Couldn't get away fast enough.'

Angel nodded.

'Who is this Lady Blessington?'

'She's a long-standing friend of Alicia. At least I thought she was. Oh dear! She has visited Alicia several times lately. I was in the garden, enjoying the sun, this afternoon when she arrived. She waved to me as she went up the path.'

'Then what happened?'

'I sensed something was wrong. I don't like to pry, but I couldn't stop myself. There's a small gate in the privet behind the forsythia. It's a short cut between the houses. I went straight through it and up to Alicia's front door and knocked on it. I knocked very hard. And called out, so that she wouldn't be nervous. Of course, she didn't reply. I tried three times. Then I was very worried, with her being blind.'

Angel's head came up.

'Blind?'

'Registered blind. Yes. That's what makes it so worrying, Inspector, and so … so sad.'

He nodded.

'So I tried the door. It wasn't locked. I opened it a few inches and called again. Again, of course, there was no reply. I went in, still calling her name all the time so that I wouldn't startle her. She wasn't in the kitchen, so I went into the sitting-room and there she was. At first I thought she was asleep. But she didn't reply to my calls, so I went up closer to her and then I saw the blood ... on her face.'

She broke down. She removed the spectacles and wiped her damp cheeks.

Angel wanted to pat her on the shoulder but restrained himself. After a few moments, he said: 'Then you dialled 999?'

She nodded

'Mmmm. Could you describe this Lady Blessington for me?'

She put a hand to a corner of her mouth, her fingers shaking like a dying butterfly.

'Erm. She was very ordinary. With blonde hair, crimped like we used to do. She was wearing a fussy, light blue dress and a big yellow straw hat trimmed in matching blue.'

'Shoes? High-heeled shoes?'

'No. Flatties. Summer shoes. White, I think.'

'Of course. And a handbag. What colour?'

'White.'

'Right,' he said decisively. 'How old would Lady Blessington be?'

'Deceptive, Mr Angel. She wasn't young. I never got a close look at her face. They say you can tell from the wrinkles round the eyes, don't they? She was a strange woman. Hmmm. Somewhere between forty and sixty, I suppose. That's about as close as I can get, I'm sorry.'

'That's all right,' he grunted. 'Why do you think this Lady Blessington would murder Mrs Prophet.'

'I have absolutely no idea. She seemed such a pleasant woman.'

'You met her then?'

'Not exactly. No. Seen her a few times. She always waved if I was in the garden. Her name came up one day when I was chatting to Charles … that's Mr Prophet. She was an old friend of Alicia's from way back. Charles didn't seem to care for her much.'

Angel pulled a face, sighed and rubbed his hand hard across his mouth. He thrust his hand into his pocket for his mobile. 'Excuse me a minute,' he said as he opened it, tapped in a number, then put it to his ear.

'What can you tell me about the taxi driver?' he asked.

She shook her head.

'Never saw the driver. Saw the taxi, though.'

'Anything distinguishing about it?'

'I should have had my contact lenses in. They dry out in this heat, you know. The taxi was big, like those in London, and black.'

He wrinkled his nose.

'Never mind. We'll find it.'

There was a voice from the mobile.

'Excuse me,' Angel said to her and put the phone to his mouth.

'Ahmed. Has Trevor Crisp turned up?'

'No, sir'

His lips tightened against his teeth.

'Find him,' he snapped. 'I want him urgently. Now Ahmed, I want you to see if we have anything on a Lady Blessington. And a Charles Prophet, solicitor, of Creesforth. Got that?'

'Yes, sir.'

'Then I want you to find the taxi driver who dropped a woman in a blue dress and/or collected her from this address, 22 Creesford Road, this afternoon. You'll have to ring round the taxi firms a bit smartish. All right? Phone me back when you get anything. You might get Scrivens to give you a hand.'

'Got it, sir,' Ahmed said promptly.

Angel closed the phone and dropped it into his pocket. He looked across at Mrs Duplessis. 'Did you know the

Prophets well?' He quizzed, meanwhile thinking that it was time that he met the man.

'I like to think I was a … good neighbour. I, sort of, tried to keep an eye out for her, particularly in regard to any strangers who might have called when Charles was out at work. They have a young woman who comes for a few hours a week. Does the cleaning, washing, tidying round and so on.'

'Has she been in today?'

'Don't think so. Haven't seen her.'

'I'll need a name and address.'

'Her name is Margaret. I'm not sure what her surname is. She lives in the top flat in that block at the top of Mansion Hill. She seems a willing enough girl … pleasant and that. Don't know anything more about her. Charles will be able to—'

'Of course. Happily married, the Prophets, were they?'

Mrs Duplessis looked taken aback, as if he had asked something improper.

'As happy as any married couple, I should say,' she said firmly.

Angel thought about her reply. It sounded genuine.

'Been blind long, had she?' he asked carefully.

'A few years, I think. It happened before we moved here – a big shock to her, and to him. Fell down some stairs. Hit her head on a step.'

With raised eyebrows, he nodded, thinking he had got enough information from her to be going on with. 'Thank you, Mrs Duplessis.'

CHAPTER THREE

Dr Mac, dressed in whites, and carrying his case and a plastic bag, plainly containing samples of evidence, was coming out of Number 22. Angel waited at the front gate for him.

'Ah, Michael,' Mac said. 'This your case?'

'Aye, for my sins.'

Mac smiled.

'Hear you've got an eyewitness?'

'Looks like it,' Angel sniffed. 'We'll see.'

A woman walking a Yorkshire terrier stared at the apparition in white as she passed between them on the pavement.

'What've you got?'

Mac opened his car door and dropped his case and the plastic bag inside, then began to pull off the whites. 'A woman, aged about forty. Shot in the forehead. One bullet. Calibre .202. She was shot while sitting where she was found, on a settee, I believe. At very close range. There are powder burns on her chin and on her clothes. I have found what seems to be a human hair on her skirt.'

Angel's face brightened.

'The result of a struggle?'

'Don't think so. There don't appear to be any signs of a struggle. The woman appears to have been moderately attractive, but no clothes disarranged or anything like that, so I'd rule out any sexual motive. The downstairs seems pretty tidy; I don't think the place has been searched, so I'd also rule out robbery.'

Angel pulled a face. 'It's going to be one of those cases, is it?'

'That hair may or it may not prove to be helpful.'

Angel pursed his lips.

'Anything else?'

'Yes,' Mac said, quickly stepping out of the paper suit and rolling it into a ball. 'Peculiar. Very peculiar,' he added. He threw the roll into the back of the car, closed the door and then looked up at him. 'Yes. Strewn about the body and on the settee was … orange peel.'

Angel blinked.

'Orange peel?' he said, much louder than he had intended.

An old woman pushing a pram with a sleeping baby in it passed between them, heard Angel's outburst and stared at him as if she thought he was ready for a session with Dr Raj Persaud. He watched her until she was out of earshot.

'Orange peel?' he repeated quietly. 'Like Reynard?'

Mac nodded.

Angel's heart started pounding again. This was going to attract national interest if Reynard was responsible for the murder.

'Was a card found? Like a visiting card? His are supposed to say, "With the compliments of Reynard".'

'I didn't see anything like that,' Mac said, as he threw the rest of the discarded white suit into the back of the car. 'SOCO are still hard at it in there. They'll find it, if it's there.'

Angel started rubbing his chin. His mind began to dart off in all sorts of directions. If Reynard was suspected, the Serious Organised Crime Agency and its high ranking medico-forensic staff might bustle into Bromersley nick, take over the case, the station, the canteen and probably his office, too. He didn't want that. At the same time, they *had* expressed a particular interest in Reynard and it would be churlish not to inform them if there were clear pointers that that man might be the murderer.

Mac was now changed and behind the wheel of his car.

Angel stood on the pavement in the shade of the horse chestnut, deep in thought.

'The meat wagon's on its way, Michael. I'll send you my report later tomorrow.'

He looked up.

'Yeah, right, Mac. Thank you.'

Mac engaged the gears, pulled out of the sombre, leafy backwater and was soon out of sight.

Angel made straight for the gate to The Beeches, pushed it open and strode quickly up the path to the house door. Across the doorway was 'POLICE LINE DO NOT CROSS' tape. He reached forward, deliberately avoided the button for the doorbell and banged on the door. It took some time for the door to be answered. A detective constable in whites opened it.

'DS Taylor there?' Angel asked.

Taylor came up behind the DC.

'Come in, sir,' the sergeant said. 'We've finished the initial sweep downstairs, except for the search after the body has been removed.'

'Right. Give me some gloves.'

A white paper packet was passed to him from a plastic container.

'Nothing been moved at all?' he asked as he tore the packet open and took out a pair of white rubber gloves. 'Everything exactly as it was?'

'Except for Dr Mac's close examination of the body, sir.'

Angel nodded as he snapped the gloves on.

'Aye. Anything else?'

'He took a small piece of orange peel.'

Angel raised his head thoughtfully. He didn't say anything.

Taylor stepped back and pulled open the door.

Angel heard the humming of a vacuum cleaner. A SOCO man was upstairs sucking round for evidence. He stepped into the house. There were sterilized white sheets covering most of the floor. He followed Taylor into the sitting-room. He was slightly shocked to find the victim seated upright in the middle place of a three-seater settee. He walked tentatively over to a position in front of the fireplace and looked at her. There was a patch of dried brown blood on her forehead. Her hair was mousy-coloured and tidy; in fact there was not a hair out of place. She had clearly been a pretty woman. Her head was on one side, her eyes closed and her hands on her lap. Pieces of orange peel were strewn across the settee and several pieces on her skirt. It almost looked as if she might have peeled and eaten the orange herself, but he knew it could not have been so.

She still looked alive … although sleeping. He shuddered and briefly felt cold. The hair on the back of his neck stood on end. He had seen so many bodies, but he felt he would never get used to death, especially murder. He turned away.

Taylor had been was standing in the doorway, watching the inspector taking in the scene.

He came up to him.

'Peculiar, sir. Isn't it?'

Angel nodded and rubbed his chin.

They both looked at the figure sitting on the settee.

After a moment, Angel said: 'Did you find anything like a business card on or around the body, Don?'

Taylor frowned.

'No, sir. Nothing like that.'

'Any doors or windows forced?'

'No, sir. Back door closed but unlocked. Front door ajar. Several windows open.'

Angel shook his head censoriously.

'Well, sir, it is a warm day.'

He nodded then turned away. He found the kitchen. Everything spotless and cleared away. On the draining board at the sink, he spotted a small pile of coins neatly placed on top of a five pound note.

He turned to Taylor and pointed to them.

'What's this, Don?'

'Dunno, sir. Just as we found it. Six pounds, fifty-six pence.'

Angel stood pensively. He wondered if it meant that the murderer was honest? Unusual. Was it likely that a titled lady might be up to murdering somebody for money, but above taking six pounds odd after they were dead?

He found a door leading out of the kitchen.

'That's a pantry, sir,' Taylor said.

Angel opened it and found a large storage room. It looked clean, well-stocked and everything seemed in order. At the end of the room was a fridge. He stepped inside and accidentally kicked something. He looked down and there were two shopping bags overflowing with groceries.

He looked back at Taylor, with eyes narrowed.

'That's just as it was, sir. I don't know why.'

Angel nodded. He strode over the tops of the shopping bags and made the few paces down to the fridge. He opened the door, looked inside, observed that it contained nothing unusual. He checked the 'use by' date on a container of milk, replaced it and closed the door.

He returned to the entrance hall followed by Taylor. Together they went upstairs and looked round all the rooms. Angel saw nothing that was remarkable. They made their way downstairs. At the bottom he turned to Taylor.

'Don, I want you to look out for any reference at all to a Lady Blessington. We desperately need her address. She's our number one suspect. In fact, she's our only suspect. Letters, cards, any mention of her at all, I want to know about it. Might be in the victim's address book. The poor woman was blind, so she may not have used such a thing. The description of Lady Blessington is that she's of medium height, between forty and sixty and last seen in a powder blue dress, described as "fussy". I'm not sure what that means in this context. OK?'

'Right, sir.'

There was a knock at the door. Taylor opened it. It was DS Crisp.

Angel's mouth tightened.

'I want you, laddie!' Angel bawled before Crisp had chance to say anything.

Crisp knew he was in trouble.

Angel turned back to Taylor. 'I must get away, Don. I'll see you tomorrow.'

'Right, sir.'

The door closed.

DS Crisp was a clean-shaven, dark-haired man, much admired by the ladies, particularly by WPC Leisha Baverstock who was on the strength of Bromersley force. He was always very smartly turned out. Tidy hair. Suit sharper than a broken vodka bottle.

Angel's face flushed.

'Where the hell have you been?' he bawled, when they were alone. 'Ahmed has been trying to contact you all day. There's a murder come in. I needed you. I need every man I can get!'

'I know, sir.' He protested. 'I know. I've been phoning you. Every opportunity I had, but you were always engaged. I got called out to a drunk who was causing a disturbance in The Feathers.'

Angel sighed.

'So what?'

'Then I got buttonholed by the super. He pulled me in to attend a briefing with some "uniformed" about Reynard.'

Angel blinked.

He always found that whenever Crisp went missing and then eventually turned up, he always had a truly magnificent explanation.

'Reynard? What about him?'

'You know, sir. The murderer who always leaves a calling card behind.'

'I know all about his MO,' he bawled. 'What about *him*?'

'Information received that he was in the area, sir. It was on the front page of the *Yorkshire Mercury*. Supposedly been in Leeds last night. A man was murdered.'

'How do they know? Nobody knows what he looks like, do they?'

'No, sir. But that's what it said.'

Angel's eyebrows had shot up. He hadn't heard. That *was* unexpected.

'And what was the point of the briefing?'

'To raise the profile of Reynard, sir, and enlist our co-operation. A CDI from SOCA rolled in. They're marshalling a big operation to try to net him, as they believe there's every possibility of his turning up around here sometime.'

Angel had had enough of the banter, and he rather wanted to get away from thoughts about Reynard being in or even near Bromersley. Crisp, as usual, had delivered an almost plausible explanation. It would be time-wasting to push the argument any further. Time was precious. There was too much at stake.

Angel sighed and shook his head. He knew he'd been beaten.

'There's a woman called Margaret,' he said quickly. 'I've been told she does some cleaning for Prophets and lives in the top flat at the top of Mansion Hill. Find out where she was today … if she was at the Prophets' house at all. And what she can tell you about the relationship between the murdered woman and her husband. And anything else that might be helpful. See if she knows of the whereabouts of Lady Blessington … her home address and so on. And keep in touch. OK?'

'Right, sir.'

'Any questions?'

'No, sir.'

'Well push off then, lad. See if you can make up for all the time you've already wasted!'

Angel's mobile rang.

'Right, sir,' Crisp said, then he ran down the crazy-paving path to his car.

Angel took out his mobile as he watched the young sergeant reach the gate. Although he couldn't see his face, he knew Crisp would be laughing his socks off at him.

He sighed as he answered the phone. 'Angel.'

'It's Scrivens, sir. Ahmed says to tell you that there's nothing known on the NPC about Lady Blessington or Charles Prophet.'

'Right,' Angel grunted.

'But I've traced the taxi driver. His name's Bert Amersham. He picked up Lady Blessington just before two o'clock outside Wells Street Baths and took her to 22 Creesforth Road. He then brought her back to the baths an hour later. I spoke to him on the phone. He said he thought there was something wrong when he took her back. She seemed agitated.'

'Hmmm. Right, Ed,' Angel said urgently. 'Wells Street Baths? There's a job for you, then. Find Lady Blessington.'

Scrivens hesitated.

'Where would I start, sir?'

Angel blew out an impatient sigh.

'I don't know. You're the detective. You could start at the top of the Blackpool Tower, the Hanging Gardens of Babylon or Number Ten, Downing Street. Personally, I would start where the taxi driver said he had dropped her. Now stop wasting time. She's our number one suspect. For God's sake get out there and find her!'

Angel closed the phone, shoved it in his pocket, and walked briskly down the path to his car.

He must get to the husband, Charles Prophet, before the poor man heard the tragic news from some other source.

He saw Gawber walking on the pavement. He was carrying a clipboard. They met at the front gate.

'Nobody saw anything of anybody arriving or leaving Number Twenty-two, sir,' Gawber said.

Angel's jaw tightened. He rubbed it.

'Hmmm. They never do.'

'There was plenty of gossip.'

'Oh, yes?' he said knowingly.

'Yes. The women had plenty to say about Mr Prophet. All good though. He comes out *very* well. The perfect husband. The next best thing to Johnny Depp.'

Angel's eyebrows shot up. 'Charles Prophet: Mother Teresa in Y-fronts, eh? Loaded with money. Stuck with a woman who is blind.'

Gawber nodded wryly. 'That's about what they're saying.'

Angel grunted and then said, 'I've still got to tell that poor man about his wife.'

Gawber was aware that it had to be done.

'Anybody see Lady Blessington?' Angel asked.

'A woman in the house opposite, The Larches, Number Eighteen, says she saw a taxi arrive about two, and a woman in blue get out. She's seen her before, a couple of times. Medium height. She thought about sixty. Strange dress. Couldn't get any more detailed description. Nobody else saw anything.'

Angel wrinkled his nose.

'What's strange about a blue dress?'

Gawber shrugged.

'You'd better get after her. I've already set Scrivens on to start at Wells Street Baths, that's where the taxi picked her up and dropped her, but why Wells Street Baths, I wonder?'

He squeezed the lobe of his ear between finger and thumb.

'What attraction could an Olympic-sized swimming pool possibly have for a middle-aged titled lady who is most probably a murderer?' Angel mused.

'Swimming, sir,' Gawber said innocently.

Angel frowned.

'Swimming?' he growled. 'Well do the crawl and find her then. Smartish!'

CHAPTER FOUR

The highly polished brass plaque read, 'Prophet and Sellman, Solicitors'.

Angel sighed. He pushed open the glass door and walked into a small waiting-room where a pretty young woman was working at a computer. She glanced up at him and smiled. He looked at her more closely. She *was* a good-looker. He liked what he saw. He pulled out his warrant card and said: 'I must see Mr Charles Prophet on a matter of great urgency, please.'

She stood up and peered at the card. He noticed her tiny waist and long legs. He wondered why there were so few beautiful girls in the force.

She read the name out aloud.

'Detective Inspector Michael Angel?'

She had a voice like an angel, and made it sound as if she was referring to somebody terribly important.

'That's right, miss,' he said with a smile.

His eyes drifted down to the third finger of her left hand. There was no wedding ring showing. He breathed in deeply, pulled in his stomach and stuck out his chest.

She looked at him and smiled again. He found himself smiling back. She had full Cupid's bow lips and dark mysterious eyes. He couldn't stop looking at her.

'Won't keep you a moment,' she said and deftly manoeuvred her rounded backside round the corner of the desk. He watched her float through a mahogany door to the inner office leaving a cloud of expensive French perfume and ideas that he could get six months in prison just for thinking.

He sighed as he looked round the small waiting-room. He selected a chair near the door and sat down. Then the reason for his visit came back to him. The smile on his face melted away as sight of the wood-panelled wall and the smell of wax polish brought him back to face the awful truth. He was there to investigate a murder and had to tell a man his wife was the victim. He began to consider how he was going to break the tragic news. Although he had done it several hundred times before, it didn't get easier. There was no textbook way: no magic formula. You simply said what had to be said, gently, and that was all.

The inner office door opened and the glamorous secretary came out.

'Mr Prophet will see you immediately, Detective Inspector,' she said in a voice that would have stirred Cecil B. DeMille, if he had still been around.

Angel stood up.

'Thank you.'

He passed the young woman. He enjoyed a whiff of the perfume again, and then went through the door into the office.

The glamour went out and closed the door.

A well-groomed man with a tanned face and chiselled features stood up behind a desk in the centre of the office. He flashed a set of ivories, which Burt Lancaster's dentist would have been proud of, stretched out a hand and said, 'Inspector Angel? Charles Prophet. Very pleased to meet you. What can I do for you? My secretary said it was on a matter of great urgency.'

It was a firm handshake, the sort Angel liked.

Angel looked into the ice-blue eyes and was not a bit surprised that he was popular with all his lady neighbours.

'It is, sir,' Angel said and licked his lips.

Prophet's face changed.

'Please sit down.'

'Thank you, sir,' Angel said. 'You are Charles Prophet, married to Alicia Prophet and you do live at 22 Creesforth Road?'

'Yes?' he said. He started looking worried.

Angel certainly had the man's full attention. He took in a breath and said, 'I have some very bad news, sir. You need to prepare yourself.'

Prophet's face changed. He sat down. 'Yes?'

Angel waited only a moment and then said, 'This afternoon we had a 999 call from your neighbour, Mrs Duplessis. Police officers attended and found your wife, dead on the settee. She had been shot.'

Prophet stared across the desk at him.

'No,' he said quietly. His eyes closed and his mouth dropped open. He breathed in and then out very deeply. It was a very big sigh.

His breathing became heavy.

'My poor, dear Alicia,' he muttered. 'Did she suffer?'

'No, sir. Death would be instantaneous.'

'You know she was blind?'

'We know *now*. Yes.'

His eyes opened.

'How did it happen? How will I cope?' he asked tearfully. 'Who did this dreadful thing? Why ever would anyone want to hurt her? What happened? How will I manage without her?'

He reached out to a jug on a silver tray and poured some water into a tumbler. With shaking hands took a few sips from the tumbler.

Eventually Angel said: 'I was hopeful that you could tell us who might have murdered her.'

Prophet held the tumbler, looked down and shook his head.

'Unless it was a caller at the door? We were constantly hounded by people selling things.'

'No. We don't think it was a casual caller. However, a woman was seen leaving the scene.'

Prophet looked up.

Angel went on: 'Your next-door neighbour, Mrs Duplessis, saw a woman in a fussy blue dress. She said that her name was Lady Blessington.'

Prophet leapt to his feet. His eyes were blazing.

'Yes. Yes! Lady Blessington. Damn that woman. It would be her. It all fits.'

Angel stared at him.

'What fits?'

'That woman,' Prophet stormed. 'She's been trying to insinuate herself into an unwanted and unsought friendship with my wife for six months or so now.'

Angel licked his lips.

'Why would she do that?'

'I'm sorry to have to say it, Inspector, but for money. As far as I can tell, she's a forgotten member of the aristocracy. Apparently, my wife and she were … acquaintances years ago. I think she must have married an impecunious lord, and is now a hard-up widow. I kept trying to warn my wife against her, but Alicia, dear Alicia, wouldn't listen.'

He slumped back down in the chair. He buried his head in his hands.

'I told her time and again she should give her a wide berth.'

'Was Lady Blessington trying to extract money from your wife?'

'Yes.'

'And you think that … that … some dispute may have broken out and … in the course of it, she shot your wife?'

'Yes.'

Angel agreed. At the moment it did seem to be the most likely possibility. He rubbed his chin.

'Can you tell me,' Angel began, 'on the settee, where your wife was found there was the peel of an orange. It was sort of spread about, untidily. Looked like the peel of a perfectly ordinary, fresh orange. Can you explain that? Did your wife like oranges?'

'Really? How extraordinary. Yes, she liked oranges, Inspector. I can't explain the … untidiness. That was not like her. Very strange.'

'I know this is a terrible time for you, Mr Prophet. May I ask you just one more question and then I will leave you in peace for the time being.'

'Yes, of course,' he grunted.

'We need to get hold of Lady Blessington, of course. I have men out searching for her now. Do you happen to have her address?'

'No. I haven't. I have no idea where she lives. I wish I did. My wife may have it somewhere. I don't think so, somehow. Since she lost her sight, she also lost all interest in writing.'

'You've no thoughts where Lady Blessington might be at this moment?'

'No, Inspector. I hardly knew her. Didn't want to know her….'

'Right, sir. Thank you very much. We'll be going through everything, of course.'

He stood up.

Prophet sighed.

'Oh dear. Are your people at my house now?'

'I'm afraid they'll be there, possibly for a few days.'

'I'll stay at The Feathers.'

Angel nodded gently.

'It'll be best, sir. Please accept my sincere condolences. I'll be in touch with you tomorrow, sir. In the meantime if anything occurs to you as to where the missing woman might be, or if she should contact you, please phone the station.'

Charles Prophet lowered his head.

'Good morning, sir,' Gawber said.

'Ah. Come in, Ron. Good morning. Sit down. Tell me about Wells Road Baths then? Did you catch up with young Scrivens?'

Gawber sighed.

'Not much to tell, sir. Yes, Ted Scrivens is coming along fine. I took a good look round the place, the men's changing rooms, shower cubicles, tea bar and slipper baths and so on, then spoke to them in the office. They were very busy yesterday, especially in the afternoon, it being so hot. They could not remember a woman in a blue dress. The manager was very frank about it. They were run off their feet. Hadn't time to notice their own shadows.'

He nodded.

'Is there any CCTV?'

'Just the pool, for safety reasons. But nowhere else. I checked the tape last night. I didn't spot anybody on the edge or wearing a swimsuit who might have answered the description of Lady Blessington.'

Angel picked up the phone and tapped out a number.

'There's nothing else much up Wells Street … some houses,' Gawber continued. 'A newsagent's, butcher's … that's about all.'

'It might be worth going into the newsagent's,' Angel said. 'She might have popped in for something, perhaps while she was waiting for the taxi, and if she lives round there, she might be known to him. A man might remember a woman in a blue dress.'

Gawber smiled.

There was the sound of a reply from the earpiece.

'Excuse me,' he said and turned to the phone.

'Ahmed. Find out what *Burke's Peerage* says about Lady Blessington. Also, see if you can get a reference to her anywhere else … anywhere at all, on the internet or in the telephone directory, or on the voter's list at the town hall. We must find out where she lives.'

He replaced the receiver.

'I'll get onto that newsagent's, sir,' Gawber said and stood up. 'The houses up there would be too long a shot, wouldn't they?'

There was a knock at the door. Gawber opened it. It was Crisp.

'At this stage, they would,' Angel replied. 'And there's too many. But if we don't get a direct lead soon, we may have to resort to sniffing round them. Leave Scrivens up there. Tell him to scratch around. See what he can uncover. It's a long shot. Be good experience for him.'

Angel saw Crisp and said, 'Come in, lad.'

Crisp and Gawber exchanged nods.

Angel called, 'Let me know if you find out anything.'

'Will do, sir,' Gawber said as he went out. Crisp closed the door behind him.

'Sit down. Now this woman, Margaret something or other. You found her all right?'

'The name's Margaret Gaston, sir. *What* a girl,' he said with a big smile.

'Gaston. Right. Did she call at the Prophets' at any time yesterday?'

'No, sir.'

'No?' Angel said and rubbed his chin. 'What else did you find out?'

'Ah, well sir, she's a good-looking lass, about twenty-five with a great figure. She has long blonde hair, and—'

'You weren't supposed to be checking her out for the position of the next *Mrs* Crisp!'

'No sir,' he said, trying to stifle a smile. 'Well, she's got a young son aged about two and she lives on her own in this small flat at the top of Mansion Hill, number 19.'

'A one-parent family?'

'I think so, sir.'

'Aye. Go on.'

'She does a few hours a week cleaning and house-keeping for the Prophets.'

'Was she at the house at all yesterday?'

'No, sir. Monday is her day off.'

'When she's at the Prophets', who looks after her little boy?'

Crisp licked his lips.

'She didn't say, sir.'

Angel's jaw tightened.

'You didn't ask, did you?' he growled.

Crisp's eyes bounced.

'Never thought about it, sir.'

Angel shook his head. He wasn't pleased.

'Did you ask her how well the Prophets got on together?'

'Yes, sir. She said that she thought they got on well enough. She didn't know much about it, she said, because she was usually alone at the house with Mrs Prophet during office hours when Mr Prophet was out, at the office.'

'Did she ever see Lady Blessington?'

'No. She said she'd never heard of her.'

Angel frowned, then his eyebrows shot up and his mouth dropped open.

'Really? Mrs Prophet never spoke to her about the woman?'

'Apparently not, sir. That's what she said, anyway. On reflection, it does seem a bit strange. You'd expect her to boast a bit about knowing a titled lady.'

Angel frowned.

'Wasn't she ever there when Lady Blessington called?'

'Couldn't have been, sir.'

'Don't you think that's odd?'

Crisp considered the question.

'It could just be a coincidence.'

Angel squeezed an earlobe between finger and thumb. He wasn't happy about it. He'd never believed in coincidences, not in the murder business.

'No good asking you if she knew the address of the mysterious Lady Blessington then, is it?'

Crisp shook his head.

The phone rang. Angel reached out for it. It was a young PC on reception.

'There's a woman here, sir. Reporting a lodger gone missing. She sounds worried. Inspector Asquith is at the hospital having his sinuses washed out or something. I don't know quite what to do with her.'

Angel would have liked to have told him; instead, he sighed.

'Right, lad. Ask the lady to wait. I'll get DS Crisp to see her.'

He replaced the phone and turned to Crisp.

'Nip up to reception. A woman reporting a misper. See if you can sort it out smartish. Then come back here.'

'Right, sir,' Crisp said and dashed out of the office.

Angel picked up the phone and tapped in a number. It was soon answered. It was DS Taylor.

'I take it you are still at 22 Creesforth Road? Have you found anything that would indicate the address of this Lady Blessington, Don. We can't find it anywhere. Nobody seems to know.'

'Nothing yet, sir.'

'Is there anything in the place that might help us? A letter, a photograph?'

'There is a drawer with a lot of loose photographs in a drawer in the sitting-room. They are not in an album. They might include a picture of her ladyship.'

'Aye. Right. That'd be something to be going at. I'll send round for them. And have you come across a cheque book or anything that would indicate where Mrs Prophet banked?'

'Yes sir. The Northern Bank, Market Street.'

'Right lad. Thank you.'

He replaced the phone. There was a knock at the door. It was Ahmed.

'Yes, lad. What is it?'

'Lady Blessington isn't in *Burke's Peerage*, sir. There's a Blessing, and a Blessingham, but no Blessington.'

Angel nodded.

‘And she’s not in the phone book, sir, or in the voter’s list at the town hall, or on the internet. Do you want me to look anywhere else?’

‘No, Ahmed. I think it is fast becoming clear that our Lady Blessington is no lady, in *every* sense of the word. We are looking for a woman who is a murderer, untitled, in a powder-blue fussy dress, has blonde hair and appears to be between the ages of forty and sixty.’

Ahmed nodded, but couldn’t think of anything useful to say. He turned to go.

‘Just a minute,’ Angel said. ‘There’s summat else. Go to 22 Creesforth Road and collect a bundle of photographs from SOCO and bring them here. On your way back, I want you to call in at the Northern Bank. Tell the manager we are looking into the murder of Mrs Alicia Prophet and get a copy of statements of her account for the last 12 months and look sharp about it.’

Ahmed dashed off.

The phone rang again. It was Crisp in reception. ‘Sorry to bother you, sir. About this misper. This lady is worried about one of her tenants. He’s been missing a month. Would you have a word? Incidentally, she owns the flats at the top of Mansion Hill, where another of her tenants is Margaret Gaston.’

Angel pulled an unhappy face. He rubbed his chin. He’d plenty on his plate. He really didn’t want to get involved.

‘All right, bring her down. Let’s get on with it.’

CHAPTER FIVE

'I am Detective Inspector Angel. Please sit down, Mrs-er …' Angel said.

'Thank you. My name is Elizabeth Reid, *Mrs* Elizabeth Reid,' the tubby Scottish lady said in a raw Glaswegian dialect.

'I understand that you lease out flats in that block at the top of Mansion Hill and that one of your tenants has gone missing, Mrs Reid? Tell me about him.'

'Yes, Inspector. A man came to me about three months ago. He was after a bedsit. Mr Harold Henderson his name was. I fixed him up with one on the top floor, number twenty. He seemed a reliable, clean-looking man. He paid me a month's rent in advance. I made out a rent book in his name. He's now overdue. I collect, normally on a Tuesday. I've called the last four Tuesdays. He wasn't in. He's never in. I thought it was odd, so this morning, when he didn't reply, I used my key to take a look … see what was happening, you know. When I got inside, it was untidy, sink full of pots, dirty clothes all over the place. That's usually what I find with single men … nothing cleaned or dusted. It looked like he hadn't been there for weeks … like deserted!'

Angel sniffed. It didn't seem to him to be particularly significant. 'Don't you think he could have taken a holiday?' he said.

'If he has, I don't think he took any clothes with him.'

Angel rubbed his chin. Men don't need much. He could have bought a clean shirt and underwear as he went along.

'Another funny thing,' she continued. 'He's moved all the furniture round. He's put the table by the window and he's moved the bed to the middle of the room. I ask you, who sleeps in a bed in the middle of a room?'

Angel raised his head. His eyes narrowed.

'Bed in the middle of the room?' he said.

'That's right,' she said. 'It's crazy, Inspector, isn't it?'

He looked at Crisp. 'Come on, laddie. We must have a look at this.'

They were at the flats in a few minutes and climbed the three uncarpeted flights of stairs following Mrs Reid. She led them onto the top floor, along the short landing to a door with the printed plastic numbers, two and zero, gold on black, stuck to the top of the door. She produced a bunch of keys and unlocked the door.

Angel went in first. He looked round. It was an untidy room with a small window looking over some of the roofs of houses. The furniture was utilitarian. There was a small table against the window and, as Mrs Reid had said, the bed was right in the middle of the room. The floor was uncarpeted but there was a rug the size of a small hearthrug placed at the side of the bed, so that when Mrs Reid's lodger got out of bed on a morning, his feet would naturally land on the rug and not on the cold bare wooden floorboards.

Angel crossed straight to the bed, leaned down, dragged the hearthrug away, then bent down to look at where it had been. There they were, as he expected, two very fine saw cuts, three feet apart across two floorboards. They were only visible if you knew where to look. He nodded with satisfaction and with the tips of his hands and fingernails easily managed to lift first one floorboard and then the other. He pulled the two pieces from the support of the beams and handed them to Crisp.

Mrs Reid stood close by and looked on open-mouthed. 'Goodness gracious me,' she said.

Angel immediately saw the reason for the freshly made hiding place. It was stuffed with Bank of England £20 and £50 notes bundled in green Northern Bank wrappers.

Crisp's eyes glowed.

'There must be thousands, sir.'

'Aye,' Angel said. He reached into his pocket and took out his mobile. He opened it and dialled a number.

'Goodness gracious me,' Mrs Reid said again.

'Shall I count it, sir?' Crisp said.

'No. Don't touch any of it. There'll be some prints on the wrappers, and I want them clean, clear and indisputable,' he said heavily. 'Then it can be moved and counted.'

Another 'Goodness gracious me,' escaped from Mrs Reid, who then said. 'What about my Mr Henderson, Inspector? Wherever can he be?'

Angel nodded towards the cache of money.

'Don't worry about him, Mrs Reid. We'll find him. And if we don't find him, he'll definitely find us.'

There was a knock at the door. It was Gawber.

'No joy at that newsagent's, sir. He has no knowledge of a woman in blue. He has never seen her in his shop that he can recall.'

Angel's face assumed a grim expression. He pushed his hand through his hair.

'Lady B phoned the office for a taxi to pick her up outside Wells Street Baths, yesterday at a few minutes to two o'clock. How did she get to the baths? Did she walk it? Does she therefore live in walking distance of there? Would we able to trace her phone call to the taxi office?'

'I've left Scrivens there, sir. He's still working on it,' Gawber said.

The phone rang. It was DS Taylor of SOCO. 'I thought you'd like to know, sir, about that hair we found on the victim's skirt.'

'Yes Don,' Angel said, his face brightening.

'We've got a match, sir, but I'm sorry to say it's that of her husband, Charles Prophet.'

Angel wrinkled his nose. That was a big disappointment to him. 'Right. Thank you very much, Don.'

'But there's something else,' Taylor said. 'Don't know whether it's good news or bad. We've been through the Prophets' wheelie bin and, at the top, probably the last item put in there, were four oranges in a plain white plastic bag.'

Angel rubbed his chin. With Reynard's penchant for oranges, *that* was something to think about. 'Yes, Don?'

'Not likely to be from a supermarket. They were in a plain white plastic bag … probably came from a shop or a market stall.'

'Yes, but are there any dabs on it?' he asked urgently.

'Only smudges and strips: nothing we can use.'

'Oh,' he growled.

'There's something else, sir. The sample peel we took from the victim's skirt on the settee is the identical variety and the same maturity as the oranges in the wheelie. Therefore it would be reasonable to assume that there had been five oranges in the bag originally and that one of them was consumed by the murderer, Reynard.'

Angel felt a slight, cold tremor run up his back at the very mention of the name as he thought that he might be so close to identifying and arresting that infamous man.

'Pity you couldn't have managed a print off the bag,' Angel said. 'It would have been a big step forward.'

'Sorry sir,' Taylor said.

Angel thanked him, replaced the handset and brought Ahmed and Gawber up to speed with SOCO's news.

Then he said: 'Ron, Nip up to Creesforth Road. Ask Don Taylor for that bag and then go round the town. See if you can find a fruiterer in town or on the market who sold a man five oranges in a bag like that, yesterday, Monday. I know it's a long shot, but you never know.'

'Right, sir,' Gawber said and went off.

Angel watched the door close.

Ahmed came up to the desk. 'Can I do anything, sir?'

Angel smiled. He liked the lad's enthusiasm.

'Yes. Fetch me a cup of tea.'

'Right, sir,' he said eagerly, and dashed off out of the room.

Angel reached out for the phone. He tapped in SOCO's number. He wanted to speak to DS Taylor.

'Ron, I want you to send a fingerprint man up to Flat 20, Mansion Hill. There's an impressive amount of fun-time money under the floorboards, and I want to know where it has come from. It wants fingerprinting, counting and depositing in the station safe. Trevor Crisp is hanging on there for you. All right?'

He hung up and pushed the swivel chair backwards and gazed up at the cream ceiling with the grey dust marks round the rose and the electric flex that came down holding the white plastic lampshade. He rubbed the lobe of his ear between finger and thumb.

There were many things that didn't make sense in this murder case. This orange business was wacky. Why would Reynard buy five oranges, murder somebody, peel one, throw the peel over her, eat it and throw the other four away?

'Come in. Come in,' Harker squawked. 'Sit down. Sit down.'

Angel knew he was in a bad mood, by the speed he spat out his instructions and the pitch of his voice.

Angel pulled up a chair and looked across the desk at the superintendent. His bushy ginger eyebrows made him look like one of the uglier Muppets. And he didn't look well. His face was the colour of an outside loo and there was that lingering smell of TCP. He always smelled of the stuff when he was out of sorts.

'Now, what's all this about the Prophet woman being murdered by Reynard?' Harker said challengingly.

Angel blinked. He must have been talking to SOCO. He didn't know that Harker was yet familiar with the finding of orange peel at the crime scene. 'I'm not sure that she was, sir,' he replied carefully.

'Orange peel over her body, isn't that the MO?'

'Not strewn about the place like this was, sir. The case notes of his two latest victims say that the orange peel was put in a relatively tidy pile, in one case on a table, and the other, a chair arm. Also, there was a printed card about, saying, "With the compliments of Reynard". SOCO have found no sign of a card.'

'I know all about that,' Harker said leaning back in his chair and flaring his nostrils.

At that angle, his nose looked like the entrance to the Dover to Calais tunnel.

'Nevertheless,' Harker continued. 'SOCA should be advised. We want a quick clear up, and they've been making a special study of Reynard. They've got specialist officers. They maybe could clear this up in no time. Also, I heard that in that Merseyside murder, all the motor expenses for the two weeks they were there, were put down to SOCA. Saved Liverpool CID over six thousand pounds. Helped their quarterly budget no end.'

Angel frowned as he ran his tongue round his mouth desperately thinking of what to say. Then it came to him. He looked up.

'Yes, but SOCA sent in a Chief Super in that South Hixham case, sir. A woman called Macintosh. Eighteen stones she was. You may know her? I heard from a DI up there that she had the station running round like rabbits. Made everybody jump. *Everybody*, except the Chief Constable. And it was the Chief Constable who eventually had to bring things to a halt. The regular police work had been brought to a standstill. She had cancelled all leave and rescheduled the shift system, and they had had to pay out thousands in overtime. And despite all the upset and palaver throughout the station, they still didn't catch Reynard.'

Harker frowned. 'Hmmm,' he said slowly. He was thinking.

Angel looked at his eyes. He had slowed him down. He was weighing the pros and cons. His pupils were bouncing and moving from side to side. The cogs were moving like a Heath Robinson time machine.

Angel concealed a smile and turned away.

After a few moments, Harker said: 'Very well, as you are certain it isn't Reynard, we needn't bother SOCA. That's all I really wanted to know. Carry on then.'

Angel looked across at him. He wasn't happy. What Harker had said was not exactly correct. If Reynard proved to be the murderer of Alicia Prophet, and SOCA had *not* been advised early in the investigation, SOCA would be furious and a big rocket would be sent from them to the Chief Constable. Somebody would be in trouble. But it wouldn't be Harker. Oh no. He'd simply say that he, Angel, had misled him.

He closed the door.

Ahmed passed two envelopes across the desk. One was a large A4 Manilla with the one word, EVIDENCE, printed across it in red, and a smaller one bearing the name and logo of the Northern Bank PLC in small black letters in the corner.

'The bank was a bit funny about releasing Mrs Prophet's statements to me, sir,' Ahmed said. 'Until I showed my ID and told them about her death.'

'They would be, and a good job too,' Angel said as he slit open the envelope from the bank with a penknife.

Ahmed nodded, went out and closed the door.

Angel took the bank statements out of the envelope. There were twelve sheets. He looked at them carefully. There hadn't been much activity in the account, but he did note that for the past six months a regular amount of £1,000 a month had been deducted from her balance. There was no payee's name; the entries simply said that the withdrawals were in cash. He checked them over again then wrinkled his nose. That six thousand pounds needed some explanation.

He turned to the thicker envelope. He opened the top and peered inside. It contained photographs, mostly black and white, in all sizes. He closed the flap and put the envelope back on the desk. He looked at it thoughtfully for a few seconds and then reached out a hand to it and tapped it twice with the fingertips. He had made a decision. He stood up. The phone rang. He raised his eyebrows as he reached out for the receiver. It was Harker.

'There's a treble nine,' he said urgently. 'A man's body found in a skip down the side of The Three Horseshoes, off Rotherham Road.'

Angel pulled a face. His pulse began to race. Another body. Here we go again. Would it never end? Another murder, and he'd quite enough on his plate.

'Reported by a workman, a James Macgregor,' Harker added. 'He's waiting there on site.'

'Right, sir,' Angel said, then he phoned SOCO, Dr Mac and Gawber. He passed on the information and instructed them to make their way to the crime scene A.S.A.P. He also advised Ahmed of the recent developments and instructed him to tell Crisp to join him as soon as the money under the floorboards in the flat had been dealt with and deposited in the station safe. He then grabbed the thicker of the two envelopes and dashed down the green-painted corridor to the rear door exit that led to the station car park.

Five minutes later, the white SOCO van, Dr Mac's car and Angel's BMW arrived at The Three Horseshoes in quick succession. The pub was on the corner of the Mansion Hill and Rotherham Roads, not the best part of Bromersley. It had a small car park on one side of it, but locals would take the shortcut between the two roads, across the car park and park behind the pub, thus cutting off the corner and saving half a minute or so walking round the front of the pub.

Angel parked on the street. He noticed a small skip in the car park by the rear wall of the pub and advanced determinedly towards it. The green-painted skip had the words 'For hire' and an 0800 telephone number stencilled in white on each side. As he got nearer he could see that it was three-quarters filled with stone, dust, bricks, plasterwork and builder's debris. At one end, there appeared to be a bundle of brown rags with a man's shoe on top. That was the dead man.

SOCO were setting up blue and white tape bearing the words POLICE LINE – DO NOT CROSS, while Mac had found a bottle crate and was preparing to stand on it to lean over the skip. The car park was bathed in brilliant sunshine so extra lighting on the body was not necessary.

Angel met James Macgregor, who was in the pub drinking tea from a vacuum flask. He told Angel that he was working on some conversions in The Three Horseshoes, knocking an inside wall down to make two rooms into one and that in the course of bringing out a wheelbarrow of rubble, a few minutes ago, he had pushed it up a plank and found this body.

'Yeah. I'd noticed what I thought were some old clothes someone dumped in the skip earlier this morning, you know. People do that, you know. Get rid of rubbish in any old skip they see hanging around the streets, you know. So. Well then I didn't think anything of it. I'd tipped in a few loads before I had a closer look, and of course, it was this poor man.'

'Did you touch him?'

'Who? No. No. I snatched at his coat but soon let go when I seed him inside it, of course. Well, you would, wouldn't you?'

'What time did you finish work yesterday?'

'Five o'clock. Always finish at five, you know.'

'Was everything else as you left it?'

'Exactly. Yeah. I fetched all my tools and gear in here.'

Angel thanked him and then spoke to the landlord and his wife, who had nothing useful to add. They had had a busy but peaceful evening in the bar, and nothing unusual had occurred.

Angel nodded and came out of the back door of the pub as one of the SOCO team in standard disposable white paper overalls was snapping photographs of the pub, the skip, the body and everything else that didn't move.

Gawber arrived and came rushing across the car park.

'Do the door-to-door, Ron. All I've got is a dead man in a brown suit, who wasn't here at 5 o'clock yesterday afternoon.'

'Right, sir,' Gawber said and set off back the way he'd come.

Angel turned back to the skip.

Mac was in the skip, kitted out in the white paper overalls, hat, rubber boots and gloves. He hovered over the body.

Angel called over to him. 'Cause of death, Mac?'

The doctor wasn't pleased. He muttered something including an expletive he'd no doubt learned in his student days while washing pots for beer money in a Glasgow pub.

'Didn't quite catch it, Mac,' Angel said knowingly.

'I don't know the cause of death yet,' he snapped testily. 'Give me a chance! Wound to the chest. Lot of blood around. Lot of bruising. He's been badly knocked about. Might take me a day or so.'

Angel's eyes narrowed.

'Nasty. Sounds like a gang-type attack, more than one assailant?'

There was a pause before Mac snapped out his reply.

'Don't know. Ye'll have to wait.'

Angel looked away. That was the problem – he couldn't wait. He looked back at the body and tried to get a square look at the face. Mac had turned the head over to pull up the eyelids. There were blue bruises to the forehead and the cheeks. There was blood dried on his lips, which also seemed swollen. Nobody could ID him in that state.

Angel wasn't prepared to hang around.

'Look in his pockets, Mac,' he said patiently. 'I need to know who he is.'

Mac had just put something in a small transparent packet. He zipped across the top of it to seal it, wrote on it and put it in a white valise over his shoulder.

'Aye. All right. Anything to shut you up.'

He pulled the body round more easily to reach the inside pocket. He reached inside found something. He brought it out, carefully holding it by the edges.

'I think I've found ye a cheque book.'

Angel's face brightened.

'Great.'

Mac opened the cover. 'It's of the Northern Bank. In the name of Simon Smith. Will that do ye?'

'Thanks, Mac.'

CHAPTER SIX

'Yes, I'm the Manager, Richard Thurrocks. How can I help you, Inspector?'

'Mr Thurrocks,' Angel said. 'We have just found the body of a man we believe to be Simon Smith. He had a cheque book issued by this branch with his name imprinted on it. What can you tell me about him?'

Thurrocks said: 'Oh dear. Simon Smith. Lots of Smiths. Ah yes. I met him once, I believe. Hmmm. Let me see.'

He tapped a dozen keys on the computer on the desk in front of him, then leaned back waiting for the page to come up.

'Mr Smith,' he said uncertainly. 'Did he die of natural causes, Inspector?'

'We don't think so,' Angel said heavily.

'Oh dear.'

Thurrocks looked back at the screen. 'Ah yes. Opened the account on December 17th, 2004. I remember. He sold the family business for a tidy sum. Hmm. He seems to have been slowly reducing the balance ever since.'

Suddenly the penny dropped in Angel's head and he sensed he might be on familiar ground. He looked across at Thurrocks.

'Is this the same Smith who sold his glass bottle works to an American firm?'

'I believe so.'

'For two million pounds?'

He hesitated. 'I really shouldn't say, Inspector.'

Angel's jaw muscles tightened. 'You really should,' he said glaring at him. 'This is a murder enquiry.'

'Well, yes, then,' Thurrocks said.

'What's the credit balance now, then?'

'Less than a hundred pounds.'

Angel's eyes flashed.

'Looks like you may have been robbed.'

'That's not possible,' Thurrocks said, but he was beginning to look worried. 'We have systems and procedures to protect us from fraud.'

'Well, somebody *has*.'

Angel rubbed his chin. There was something very fishy about this.

'What can you tell me about Simon Smith?'

'Not much, Inspector. Highly respectable. If I remember correctly, he had sold his business and wanted to deposit the proceeds safely for a short period while he and his family had a holiday. I don't think he actually came into the branch again. I certainly don't remember seeing him. Just a minute, Inspector. The proceeds were left on a high-rate deposit account. It would have required his written instructions to transfer it to a current account. We wouldn't have issued a cheque book without it. We must have received a letter or a signature to do that. All transactions thereafter would be conducted quite securely by cheque and post or phone. There really is no chance of fraud.'

Angel frowned. He really must see the dead man's sister again, P.D.Q.

'Can you turn up the letter?'

'Oh yes,' he said confidently. 'Excuse me a minute.'

Thurrocks went out of his office.

Angel leaned back in the leather chair. It was pretty luxurious. He banged lightly on the arm rests and thought how comfortable it was. He turned up his nose in a familiar expression as he considered that it would have been bought with the interest from many a naive soul's overdraft. He looked round the office at the plush furnishings. Momentarily, he felt quite envious. But then he liked being a detective at inspector level much more than doing bank work. Very much more. And he enjoyed catching murderers. It had become his speciality. He suddenly had a thought. He took out his mobile and tapped in a number. It was soon answered by Ahmed. He asked him to look at the notes he had made on his desk during Miss Smith's visit the day before and to give him her phone number. He said he would hold on while Ahmed looked it out. It took him a couple of minutes before he came back to the phone. He recited Miss Smith's phone number. Angel thanked him, closed the phone and recorded the number on the back of an envelope. He was pocketing the envelope as Thurrocks came back into the room. Angel noticed the man wasn't very happy. He was tapping his bottom lip and chin with shaking fingers.

'Surprising, Inspector,' Thurrocks said. 'There certainly *was* a letter. There is an entry duly recorded in the post journal, but the letter is not in the file where it should be.'

Angel frowned. He looked Thurrocks up and then down.

'Hmmm. If it turns up, I want to see it,' he said heavily.

'So do I!' Thurrocks said.

'What is the address you have for Simon Smith?'

He read it off the computer screen and Angel duly recorded it on the envelope.

'Can you remember what he looked like?'

'No. I only saw him the once. He must have looked … ordinary, conventional that is, or I would have remembered.'

'I expect the thief might well leave that small balance to avoid the more conspicuous action of actually closing the account.'

Thurrocks flopped down into his chair.

'I don't understand it,' he said, biting his nails. 'This has never happened before.'

'Tell me,' Angel said thoughtfully. 'Has anybody left your employment in recent days?'

Thurrocks shook his head slowly, then he stopped, his eyes glowing like cat's eyes in a country road. He looked across the desk at Angel.

'There was one man – Spencer,' he said excitedly. 'Spencer! Yes. That was his name. Left without working out his notice. Simon Spencer. Promising young man as well.'

'I want his full name, last address and you'll have his national insurance number.'

These were quickly supplied, then Angel phoned them through to Ahmed and told him to check on his last known address. Also to contact the national insurance office in Newcastle to see if he was claiming any state benefits.

He closed the phone and turned back to Thurrocks.

'If anyone comes in the bank to attempt to withdraw any more from this account, phone me and try to detain them. In the meantime, I will be setting up other inquiries. And I would ask you to keep this confidential Mr Thurrocks, except, of course, from the bank's directors. I wouldn't want your staff or any outsider to know of the police's interest in Spencer yet. All right?'

'Right, Inspector.'

He took his leave and returned to the BMW.

He stood uncertainly, at the car door. There was so much to do, he didn't know where to turn next. He was anxious to know if SOCO or Dr Mac had uncovered any clues at the scene. And he also wondered if Ron Gawber's house-to-house had unearthed anything. He needed to keep on that murder while the crime scene was hot.

He got into the car and drove off towards The Three Horseshoes.

His mind was still racing. He couldn't be certain what had happened to Simon Smith. Was he lost in the Tsunami or not? According to Miss Smith, her brother had died in the Tsunami. If that was so, the body in the skip couldn't be his. If it wasn't Smith's, then whose was it? And there was another thing....

He arrived at The Three Horseshoes and parked in the car park next to SOCO's white van. A few nosy parkers had seen the police vehicles, the incident tape and SOCOs in conspicuous whites, and were hovering near the main pub door.

There was no sign of Dr Mac, nor the body in the skip. Angel crossed the car park, lifted the tape and almost bumped into Taylor. He was still in whites and, coming out of the van, was waving an email.

'Just had confirmation back from the station, sir,' Taylor said. 'The fingerprints of the dead man match those of an escaped prisoner, Harry Harrison, 36. Escaped while being transferred from Wakefield in January.'

Angel's face brightened. He nodded appreciatively. It was always good to know the identity of a victim. It cleared that up.

'And there's more, sir. They also match some of the prints on the wrappers of that hoard of money you found round the corner under the floorboards. And that money's now in the station safe.'

Angel's mouth opened in surprise. 'Harry Henderson? Aka Harry Harrison. Of course,' he said. 'I remember. He escaped in a prison transfer in January with Eddie Glazer.'

He knew of Glazer: a wicked, dangerous hard nut, inside for a long stretch for murder. Harrison was small fry. His speciality was conning old ladies out of their pension money by pretending to be an official from the water board or some official organization.

'Eddie Glazer and Harry Harrison were not in the same league,' Angel said.

'At least his mother will now know where he is at nights,' Taylor said. 'If he had one.'

Angel sighed. At least one puzzle was beginning to unravel.

'Did you count that money, Don?'

'There were two million pounds, sir.'

Angel sniffed. It was a lot of cabbage for a sloppy, tinpot conman like Harrison to come by. However did he manage it? He shook his head. Life was full of surprises.

'Where's Dr Mac?'

'He's finished here, sir. There wasn't much. The mortuary van has collected the body and gone.'

'You got anything interesting?'

'A few hairs on the corpse's suit, sir. And some dust. Blood off the outside corner of the skip. We'll be having a look at them in the lab.'

Angel nodded. Sounded promising.

'Was he killed here?'

'Dr Mac thinks so. Stabbed several times. We didn't find a weapon. We're about finished here, sir, unless you want us for anything. We'll be away in two minutes.'

'Right, Don. Thank you,' he said and turned away.

Taylor headed back into the van.

Angel saw Gawber thrusting across the car park with his head down, returning from his door-to-door calling.

'What you got, Ron?'

'Nothing, sir,' he said wearily. 'Nobody saw *anything*.'

Angel sniffed.

'Would a photograph have helped?' he asked with a smile.

Gawber's eyebrows shot up.

'Why? Do you know who it is, sir?'

'Aye. Harry Harrison.'

Gawber nodded. 'That worm,' he said indignantly.

'Never mind,' Angel said. 'How did you get on chasing the oranges?'

'I found the fruit stall on the market without any difficulty, sir. There are only a few stalls open on a Monday. The bag *was* unusual. The stallholder said he was using those bags temporarily because he'd run out of his regular brown paper printed bags.'

'Yes. Yes,' Angel said quickly. 'Did he remember selling a man five oranges, or any oranges, that's the point?'

'No, sir. He didn't.'

Angel sighed.

'But he did recall selling oranges – he couldn't be sure how many – to various women, including Margaret Gaston.

He knew her because he used to go out with her, before she got herself up the duff.'

'Margaret Gaston?' he roared in surprise. He considered the implication. 'Did he recall the time?'

'About one o'clock,' Gawber added.

Angel rubbed his chin. 'Whatever time it was, Ron. It's a certainty she couldn't be Reynard!'

'Of course.'

'Could he remember anybody else?'

'No, sir. Not by name anyway.'

Angel pulled a face and turned away. Then he suddenly looked at his watch. He ran his hand through his hair, turned back excitedly, licked his bottom lip and said, 'Look, it's almost five o'clock. I've got an urgent little job for you. Nip along smartly up the road to the office of the *South Yorkshire Daily Examiner*. I don't know what time they put that rag to bed. Speak to the assistant editor. Tell him about finding the dead body of Harry Harrison. Tell him that we are absolutely baffled. Tell him all about the case, and in particular, ask him – as a favour to me – to give the story a prominent position in the paper, and, especially remember to say that we discovered that Harry Harrison had been living in flat number twenty at the top of Mansion Hill. Specify *flat number twenty*. All right?'

'Right, sir,' he said and turned to go.

Angel grabbed him by the sleeve and said: 'And don't forget to tell him, the police are completely baffled. He'll like that. Anything that puts the police down. Huh. He'll probably put *that* on the front page!'

Gawber dashed off to his car on the street and drove away and, a minute later, the SOCO van reversed away from the skip on The Three Horseshoes car park, turned and drove onto the main road heading back towards the station.

Angel took one last glance round the car park and at the skip and then made for his car. He was just getting in when he heard the sound of an insistent car horn. He looked round. It was Crisp, anxious to get his attention. Crisp drove up next to Angel's BMW and pulled on the brake.

'Sir. Sir,' Crisp called.

'What've you doing, lad? I've been looking out for you.'

'I was staying with that money until SOCO came.'

'I have seen Don Taylor. That was two hours ago. What have you been doing since? I told Ahmed to find you—'

'He did, sir. I had to write up my notes. I came as soon as I could.'

'Write up your notes? There was very little to write up. What have you been doing?'

'Then I had lunch.'

'Lunch?' he bawled. 'How long did you take for lunch? What did you have, kippers?'

Crisp said nothing.

Angel shook his head. His jaw was set. It was pointless pursuing the matter: Crisp always had an answer.

After a few moments Angel said, 'Do you want some overtime?'

'I wouldn't volunteer for it, sir.'

Angel licked his bottom lip. He thought he knew a surefire way of changing his mind. 'Not even if it's back up on the top floor of Mansion House flats?' he said artfully.

Crisp blinked then gave him an old-fashioned look.

'Margaret Gaston's pad, sir?' he said brightly.

'No. Next door,' he said. 'Number 20.'

'Mr Prophet will see you now, Inspector,' she said holding the office door open.

Angel liked her smile, her teeth, her hair, her face, her smell and her figure. He wondered how any woman were lucky enough to have everything in such perfect form standing in what he guessed were outrageously expensive shoes.

'Thank you,' he said as he passed her and enjoyed the close brief whiff of the perfume.

Prophet was standing, leaning over the desk with his arm outstretched.

Angel transferred the envelope of photographs he had brought in with him to his left hand and shook Prophet's hand.

'Ah. Pleased to see you, Inspector. Please sit down. Are you any nearer finding my wife's murderer?'

'Frankly, no, but it is early days. There are a few questions I must ask you, Mr Prophet.'

'Of course. I realize that you let me off lightly yesterday. It was most considerate.'

Angel nodded then said, 'We aim to please. You will know that most murders are committed by their nearest and dearest?'

'Indeed, yes.'

'So we have to eliminate you absolutely from our enquiries. So I have to ask if you can account for your whereabouts yesterday afternoon.'

'Indeed, I can.'

He picked up a telephone and said, 'Karen. Will you come in here a moment, please.' He replaced the phone.

'I was at my desk, here, from one-thirty until you came yourself and broke the news at … about twenty to five. My secretary, Miss Kennedy, I am certain will confirm it.'

The door opened and Karen Kennedy came in.

'Karen,' Prophet said, 'the Inspector is asking about my whereabouts yesterday afternoon. Would you kindly tell him where I was?'

'Mr Prophet was in the office the entire afternoon, Inspector, as usual.'

'Thank you,' Angel said. 'Did he have any visitors?'

'No,' she said. 'I know that he was very busy on a particular case. There were several phone calls for him, but I managed to head them off.'

'Right. Thank you,' Angel said.

She smiled angelically and went out.

'I hope that satisfies you, Inspector.'

'Yes. Of course. Now can you think of anybody who would have wanted your wife dead?'

'No. Except, of course, Cora Blessington.' Prophet's eyes narrowed. 'I thought you had a witness, Mrs Duplessis next door. Cora was seen coming out of the house, didn't you say? I thought the case was cut and dried. It *was* Cora Blessington who murdered my wife, wasn't it?'

Angel nodded. 'It certainly *looks* like it. We just have to be very careful and quite certain, you know. You're in the legal profession, Mr Prophet. You know what it's like satisfying the law.'

Prophet sighed.

'What more do you need?'

'Motive.'

'Money, I should think.'

'Have you any proof of that?'

'No. But my wife was immensely rich, in her own right. She handed dosh out to charities like there was no tomorrow.'

Angel rubbed the lobe of his ear between finger and thumb. It sounded as if Prophet didn't know about the thousand-pound-a-month deficit in Alicia's bank balance.

'And do you think she regarded Lady Blessington as a charity?'

'Well, she certainly wasn't an asset, Inspector, was she?' he said sourly.

'Now that she's dead, who inherits her estate.'

'As her husband, I do. Do you know what I think, Inspector? I think she came to Alicia. She knew she was well off. She asked for a loan. Alicia possibly refused. She could be very stubborn if she thought she was being taken advantage of. Cora Blessington pushed Alicia as hard as she could. She visited Alicia several times over the past six months or so, and maybe asked her for money. If Alicia declined, possibly she threatened her. When Alicia finally refused, she shot her.'

Angel raised his head. 'Your wife had no deep secret that Cora Blessington could have blackmailed her with, had she?'

'No. Certainly not. The motive was straightforward. Take it from me, Inspector.'

Angel thought he could possibly be correct. A rich woman was always a target.

'I've examined your late wife's bank statements,' he continued. 'And as a matter of fact, she appears to have drawn a cheque to cash for a thousand pounds each month for the past six months.'

Angel watched him carefully. The man's eyes narrowed. His fists tightened. He thought he was going to explode.

'Can you explain where the money has gone?' Angel added.

'No. But I've got a damned good idea!'

Angel understood and was considering his next question.

Then Prophet suddenly said: 'It's outrageous. She has got to pay. You must find her and arrest her, Inspector. She has got to be punished. It's a pity they abolished hanging.'

Angel sighed and rubbed his chin.

'There's something else you might as well know, sir.'

'What's that?' he snapped.

'Whoever it was who murdered your wife on Monday, it wasn't anybody called Lady Cora Blessington: there's no such person.'

Prophet said: 'I am not really surprised, I suppose. That had passed through my mind.'

'So you must tell me all you can about her. Have you ever met her?'

'Just the once. About six months ago. Yes, must have been. I interrupted Alicia and her having afternoon tea. I thought she was quite charming in her way. I didn't know that at the time she had such evil intent, nor that she would have been able to carry it out herself.'

'And what was your wife's attitude towards her?'

'Oh, she liked her, at first, anyway. They talked about all the things my wife had enjoyed, tennis, riding, music and so on. I believe they were old school friends. I don't know which school, nor how they met up.' Prophet rubbed his chin. 'Yes. Strange that. She just popped up from nowhere and took the only person I ever cared for.'

'You wouldn't have a photograph of her, would you?'

'Shouldn't think so,' he said distastefully.

Angel passed the envelope of photographs across the desk.

'These were taken from a drawer in your sitting-room by one of my men.'

Prophet's big blue eyes opened wide.

He took the envelope turned up the flap and tipped them out onto his desk. They were typical snapshots of members of the family, on holiday, on the steps of churches, on the beach and in the garden, mostly postcard size or smaller. He leaned over the desk and pushed them around the green polished leatherette. He seemed pleased to be looking through them. Eventually he pounced on one particular square photograph in colour.

'She's *there*!' he yelled. 'Cora's there! Look!'

He picked it up, turned it round and pushed it under Angel's nose. 'There!'

Angel felt his pulse increase and that inexplicable warm hum in the chest.

Prophet pointed at an unusual-looking eccentric in a long blue dress and cream hat. Seated next to her, clearly, was the smaller figure of his wife, Alicia Prophet.

'I remember now. Of course! *I* took it. In the garden. Shortly after Alicia had introduced her to me. Alicia and Cora were having tea at the rustic table on the patio. The garden looked very nice too. The rose bushes were out. The trees were in full leaf.'

Angel strained to see the features in detail of Lady Blessington's face, but the photograph had been taken from quite a distance back and the face was partly shaded by the hat and the head of blonde wavy hair. He thought she was a big-boned woman dressed in the manner of the 1930s.

It was still a mystery, but Angel was delighted. His chest warmed with excitement and his pulse thumped noticeably. There she was: the murderer of Alicia Prophet. The name was false but, at last he was holding a photograph of the actual murderer. It was the first step towards getting a conviction. He frowned and continued to gaze at the photograph.

All he had to do was ... find the lady!

CHAPTER SEVEN

'Ah. Mrs Duplessis. Good morning. Can I have a word with you?'

'Oh?' she said peering at him. 'It's Inspector Angel, isn't it? Yes, of course. Please come in. Sit down … wherever you like.'

'Here is fine. Thank you.'

Angel took the photograph, which he had carefully wrapped in polythene, out of his pocket. 'Will you take a look at this? Do you recognize either of the two people sitting at the table?'

Mrs Duplessis took the photograph, held it to the light, adjusted her spectacles, looked back at Angel and said, 'Of course. It was taken in the garden next door. It's dear Alicia with … somebody.'

She peered at it more closely. 'They're having tea on the patio.'

Angel licked his bottom lip.

'Do you know who she is with?'

'Ah yes,' she said after a moment's hesitation. She pulled a face and added: 'It's that woman, Lady Blessington.'

'You're sure?'

'Oh yes, Inspector. Positive.'

Angel sighed and nodded.

'You couldn't mistake her,' she added. 'And that blue dress. That hat. Yes that's her.'

'And that's the woman who you saw rushing down the path just after three o'clock last Monday afternoon?'

'Without any doubt, Inspector. Yes.'

'Thank you,' he said.

He smiled. He felt good. He now had a *second* witness who provided positive ID. 'Now what can you tell me about her. You spoke to her, did you not?'

'Only briefly. She was good at the social graces. Introduced herself. Told me she was a friend of Charles and Alicia Prophet. That she and Alicia went back a long way. That she had recently caught up with her. That's about all she said.'

'Can you tell me if there was anything unusual about her … any little thing … doesn't matter how small.'

Mrs Duplessis looked blank, then shook her head.

'Well,' Angel began, 'did she have any particular mannerisms. Did she have a twitch? Did she smell of anything? The smallest thing might help me to trace her, you never know.'

'No. I can't think of anything. She always kept a good distance from me. When she shook hands, she just held out the tips of her fingers, at arm's length, very briefly. And after we had touched she pulled back and turned away, as if I had the plague.'

Angel thought about this.

'Her voice was strained, as if it pained her to speak.'

He nodded encouragingly.

'But title or no title,' she added. 'I am as clean as anybody. I am *always* washing my hands.'

'I'm sure you are,' Angel said kindly. 'Was there anything else?'

'Yes. There was something else that I noticed. Only a little thing….'

Angel nodded encouragingly.

'A matter of bad manners, really,' she said. 'Whenever I saw her come up the path, she always walked straight into the house. She never knocked and waited … like you or I would do. She didn't knock. Just barged straight in.'

'Perhaps she did that because she knew Mrs Prophet was blind. They were supposed to be good friends. Save her getting up.'

Mrs Duplessis didn't agree. She simply shook her head. She thought Cora Blessington was categorically rude.

Angel made a note of it.

'How often did you see Lady Blessington?'

'Three or four times. When I was in the garden. She would arrive suddenly, by taxi. Sail up the path. Wave and call out a greeting of some sort then dash into the house through the front door. An hour so later, a taxi would arrive, she would come out of the house, down the path to it and away.'

'Did you always see her in the company of Mrs Prophet?'

'I don't think so. Dear Alicia hardly ever came out. Her blindness made it difficult.'

'And what did she say to you about her?'

'Nothing. I don't think she ever spoke of her.'

'What did Charles Prophet say about her?'

'Can't remember him saying anything in particular. But I don't think he cared for her.'

Angel pursed his lips.

'And I didn't care for her,' she added. 'I can tell you.'

Angel nodded. He understood why.

It was ten o'clock.

Angel passed the open CID-room door on his way up the corridor to his office.

Ahmed saw him and called out: 'Good morning, sir.'

'Good morning, Ahmed,' Angel said without even glancing back. 'Have you heard from Newcastle about that address?'

'Yes, sir. Been looking out for you, sir,' he said, carrying a newspaper. 'There are a couple of things.'

'Come into my office, then. What's up?'

Angel opened the door and Ahmed followed him in.

'The address National Insurance have for Simon Spencer is 212 Huddersfield Road.'

'Right, Ahmed. That's good. Tell Scrivens I want to see him urgently, will you?'

'Yes, sir. And I've brought this to show you,' he said, unfolding the paper and putting it on the desk in front of him. It was that morning's copy of the *South Yorkshire Daily Examiner*.

Angel looked at it eagerly, his eyebrows raised.

'Ah!' he said. 'Mmmm. Done us proud. The front page. Couldn't be better.'

The headline read: '*Rubbish Skip Murder. Police completely baffled.*'

Angel smiled and quickly read the item about Harry Harrison's body being found in the skip and that he had been discovered hiding out in flat number twenty, Mansion Hill.

He smiled and put the paper down. He was as chuffed as a serial murderer let off with an ASBO.

He rubbed his chin.

He turned to Ahmed. 'While I remember, I want you to go through back copies of *Police Review* also into the NPC and see if there are any women who have been released from prison in the last three months. They may have served time for fraud, and aiding and abetting fraud. Particularly, also, if they are known to have carried handguns. All right?'

'There shouldn't be many, sir,' Ahmed said.

Angel wrinkled his nose. 'I only want *one*,' he bawled. 'One's enough!'

'Right, sir,' Ahmed said and turned to go.

'Hang on, son. There's summat else. I want a meeting of all CID on duty, in the briefing office at 16.00 hours today. DS Crisp already knows, so you needn't bother him. But spread the word. Don't miss anybody.'

'Right, sir.'

'And I'm expecting an Albert Amersham anytime now. He's a witness. When he comes, will you show him in here?'

'I got your message that you wanted to see me. I was fair worried. I never been into a police station afore, much less into an office. I'm a reight careful driver. I hope I haven't been breaking any laws or anything. And my car is regularly serviced and kept safe. Well, it has to be. You know that. Else I wouldn't get my licence.'

'It's nothing to worry about. Please sit down, Mr Amersham,' Angel said. 'Thank you for coming in so promptly.'

'Aye. Ta,' he said and looked round the little office. 'It's a darn sight posher than our dispatcher's office, I can tell you.'

'Yes. You work for A1 Taxis as a driver, don't you? Tell me about being sent to twenty-two Creesforth Road on Monday afternoon, please.'

'Well, let's see. I'd just taken a fare to the railway station to catch the 13.48 to Leeds when it came up on the RT to go to Wells Street Baths to pick up a fare for Creesforth.'

'What was your dispatcher's name?'

'Mmmm. Monday afternoon. It'd be Maisie. That's all I know her by.'

'What time would that be, Mr Amersham?'

'Well they were only just in time for the train. I saw the train leave, so it would be a few minutes to two o'clock. Say five to two. I wasn't late. I belted across town, down Wath Road, left onto to Wells Road and up to the entrance of the baths. And there she was, Lady Blessington.'

'And how did you know her name was ... Lady Blessington?'

' 'Cos she told me, when we got to Creesforth Road. Made a point of it, she did.'

'And where was she waiting exactly?'

'On the steps that lead into the baths.'

'Did you think she'd just come out of the baths then?'

'I suppose so. Niver thought about it. It was just that Maisie had said that that was where I was to pick her up from.'

'What did Lady Blessington say to you? Can you remember?'

'The usual. Just chatter, you know. The weather. It was a beautiful day. It was boiling hot.'

'Did she have any luggage?'

'She didn't have no big luggage. No suitcases or anything like that. Just a handbag, I think. I'm not sure.'

'Did you consider, that if she had been for a swim, she would have needed a towel and a swimsuit at the very least?'

Bert Amersham looked at him and blinked.

'I niver give it a thought, Inspector. I just drive a motor. I don't think about....'

'Well, did she have a bag large enough to carry, say a medium-sized towel and a swimming costume?'

'I suppose they don't take up that much room. She probably had a bag that big, I am not sure, Inspector. Sorry and all that. I remember she had a handbag. She kept her money in a handbag. I remember that. Yes. I remember that I heard it click when she closed it after she paid me.'

He sighed. 'That's all right. Now did Lady Blessington have any particular mannerism or did she behave in any way unusual?'

'We get all sorts, Inspector. All our customers are all different. She was as normal as any of them.'

'We believe that she murdered the householder, a blind lady, Mr Amersham. I am desperate to find her. You may have seen or heard something that could give me a clue as to where we might find her.'

'Wow! I didn't realize. That's a rum do.'

'Anything else you can tell me? Did she smell of anything? Did she smoke? Did she speak with an unusual accent? Did you notice any scars or marks on her face, hands or legs?'

'No, Inspector. I don't think so. None of those things. Her dress came down nearly to ground and I thought that was a bit unusual, but then again, we get all sorts.'

'You wanted me, sir,' Scrivens said.

'Yes, Ted. Come in. Close the door,' Angel said. 'There's a retired bank clerk, Simon Spencer. He's retired early. Very early. Too early! There is evidence to suggest that before he left, he got his money mixed up with the Northern Bank's. Now there's no proof yet, just a load of circumstantial. So I need you to tread carefully. The current address National Insurance have for him is 212 Huddersfield Road. Will you nip up there and ask him to be kind enough to accompany you back here to assist us with our inquiries?'

Scrivens grinned.

'Do you want him in here, or in an interview room, sir?'

'Interview room.'

Scrivens nodded and went out.

Angel picked up the phone and tapped in a number.

'It's DI Angel. Are you still at the Prophets' house?'

'Yes, sir,' DS Taylor replied. 'We broke off to attend the murder scene outside The Three Horseshoes, you know. And early this morning we swept Harrison's flat. It wasn't big, but there *were* three rooms. You told us to—'

'I'm not chasing you, Don. Just enquiring.'

'Oh? Right, sir. Well, we should be finished here this afternoon. There'll be standard samples taken from here to process.'

'Did you find anything significant at Harrison's flat?'

'No, sir. After eliminating his prints, there were no samples to take.'

Angel frowned. That meant there were no clues or DNA in the flat. He blew out a long breath. Thank God he had found the money and the prints on it!

'Right,' he said. 'In your search there ... at the Prophets', did you come across an address book?'

'Yes, sir. And a Christmas card list. I think it's in a woman's writing.'

Angel's face brightened.

'I'd like to have those A.S.A.P. And did you see a camera anywhere?'

'A camera, sir?'

'Yes. An ordinary domestic camera for taking snaps of the family and so on?'

'No, sir. No camera.'

Angel frowned.

'Right, Don. See you later this afternoon.'

He rang off.

CHAPTER EIGHT

The lift was out of order. Angel had to walk up three staircases to the third and top floor of Mansion House Flats. He started off well, but had to take the third staircase rather more slowly. When he arrived at the top, he hung onto the handrail and waited, breathing deeply several times. He stuck four fingers down the top of his shirt collar and pulled it away from his sticky neck. He sighed. He was thinking, he really would have to hold back on those meat pies and halves of *Old Peculier* at The Fat Duck for a few months. For some time, Mary had been suggesting that he took a flask, a banana and a hard-boiled egg into the office for lunch. He didn't rate that idea much. It was the sort of thing desk-bound workers do. He hadn't much time for people who pushed paper around for a living and got fat backsides from hanging onto a desk job for years on end. He had noticed a definite tightness of his trousers round the waist: maybe he'd give it serious thought. Last time they came back from Sketchley's, he had thought he had been given somebody else's by mistake.

A door banged shut on the floor below. It prompted him to move along the corridor smartly. He passed number twenty, which had been Harrison's flat, to the one next door, number nineteen. As he approached, he could hear music blaring out from inside.

He knocked on the door.

He had to wait a little time, then it was opened by a pretty young woman in a short pink house-coat, long, white uncovered legs and imitation fur slippers with rabbits heads on them. She was holding a child aged about a year. Its eyes were closed and it had a comforter in its mouth. The radio blared out loudly behind her.

Angel blinked.

The young woman had a ready smile and a bright twinkle in her eyes. 'Yes? What can I do for you?' she said.

'Miss Gaston? Margaret Gaston?' he shouted.

'Yes. Sure. Come in,' she said pulling the door open wide.

'Thank you,' he shouted over the blaring radio. It was something as loud and incomprehensible as *The Arctic Monkeys*. 'I'm Detective Inspector Angel from Bromersley Police.'

'Oh yes,' she said with a smile.

She had even, white teeth, a lovely mouth and long blonde hair hanging partly over her face like a film star of yesteryear. She looked straight into his eyes.

She carried the sleeping child with one arm, closed the door, reached down to a transistor radio on the floor, pressed a button and switched it off.

The silence was golden. Angel blew out a quantity of breath with relief.

'I've already given a statement to Trevor,' she added, looking concerned. 'Wasn't it all right?'

Angel licked his bottom lip. It had not exactly been a statement, and he was a little irritated to hear her refer to DS Crisp so familiarly. Young people talked that way. He knew it was his age.

'That was fine,' he said. 'There are some other matters.'

She looked down at the child in her arms. 'I've just got him off to sleep.'

Angel looked round the little room. It was sparsely but adequately furnished with brightly coloured plastic bricks scattered on the rug by the hearth, two teddy bears on the floor by the door, and baby clothes everywhere.

Margaret Gaston carefully put her baby in a cot, pulled up a blanket to cover him and lifted up the cot side. She kicked off the rabbit slippers across a rug on polished bare boards and flopped onto a huge leather settee and lifted her legs onto the length of it. Her bare feet showed bright red toenails. She went through the business of pulling down her housecoat to cover her underwear. Angel had noticed and tried to remember he was old enough to be her father.

'Phew! It's taken me an hour to get him off,' she said. 'Sit down.'

There was only the one easy-chair opposite, so choice wasn't a problem.

She leaned forward to the settee arm, picked up a packet of Silk Cut, shot one out, looked at Angel and waved the packet.

Angel shook his head. 'No thanks.'

She clicked a disposal lighter into life and then pulled hard on the cigarette. Then she laughed and said, 'If he doesn't want to go to sleep, it doesn't matter how tired he is, he just won't bloody go.'

Angel nodded sympathetically.

'What do you call him?'

'Carl Alexander Gaston.' She said it like making an announcement, and enjoying the way it sounded. 'What's yours?' she added taking a big drag on the cigarette.

'Detective Inspector Angel.'

'No. Your first name.'

'Michael.'

'Michael?' she said thoughtfully. 'It's a nice name. But it's so old-fashioned. Now, Carl Alexander is, sort of, cool and posh, isn't it?' she added with a smile.

'Aye, it sounds very good,' he said politely and pulled out an envelope and a ball-point. 'There are some questions I need to put to you.'

'Yes. Of course. It's dead awful about Alicia. Perfectly dreadful. However will Charles manage? Have you found out who's done it yet? Is it that Reynard that they keep on about on the telly?'

'We haven't found out yet, but we will. Now you used to clean for the Prophets didn't you?'

Her eyes suddenly flashed. 'Still do, I hope.' She said, her mouth dropping open. 'I have to have money, Michael. I get some from Social Security but it isn't anything like enough. You think he'll *still* want me to do the house and that, don't you? I've never let him down, and I wouldn't let him down now that she's … that he's on his own.'

Angel shook his head and wondered about his next question. Those long, shapely bare legs and feet moving about on the dark leather were distracting his concentration. She seemed to be unaware of it. He tried to look somewhere else.

'I do three hours a day for four days a week. I do Tuesdays to Fridays inclusive.'

'Yes. So you didn't go to the Prophets on Monday last?'

'No, Michael. Not Mondays.'

He blinked when she called him Michael. Hardly anybody ever did. He was not sure whether he objected. He let it go.

'Who looks after Carl when you're at the Prophets'?'

'I take him with me. That's what made the job so great. He's happy in his pram. He would sleep most of the time. Alicia didn't mind. She said she enjoyed the company. If he woke up, I either fed him or changed him. Alicia was very good about it.'

'Did you ever see Mr Prophet?'

'Oh yes. Not often, though. He was almost always at the office. He's a lovely man. And so handsome. It's a tragedy. When I heard about Alicia yesterday, I was gutted. I had to phone him. I had to tell him how sorry I was. And I wanted to say I'd do anything for him to help out while he got sorted. You know. More hours or different times … whatever he might have wanted, but I couldn't get past that cow at the office.'

'So you haven't spoken to him since Mrs Prophet was found dead?'

'No. Karen Kennedy wouldn't let me. She always said he was with a client. Didn't matter what time I rang, he was *always* with a bloody client.'

'You've met her – Miss Kennedy?'

'No,' she said. 'But I've seen her.'

She pulled a face.

'You don't like her?'

She pouted and said, 'She's all right, I suppose. It's just that she's always *there*. I can never even get to speak to him, when *she's* there.'

Angel rubbed his chin.

'And would you say Mr and Mrs Prophet had been happily married?'

'Oh yes, I should think so. Don't really know, do I? I didn't see much of them together, but what I saw … they both seemed to get on very well. It was difficult for him, of course, Alicia, being blind.'

He nodded.

She stubbed the cigarette out in the ashtray and said: 'You know, Michael, I told Trevor all this. Didn't he tell you?'

'Indeed, he did. But bear with me. I won't be much longer.'

'That's all right,' she said brightly. 'I'm not going anywhere. Would you like a cup of tea?'

'No, thank you.'

'There's no rush, Michael,' she said pushing a shiny clump of hair out of her eye. 'I don't mind. You know I could go for days up here and see nobody … nobody at all. And I like older men. They talk more … intelligently, you know. Women talk about their kids and schools and clothes and how expensive things are. Men talk about … well, they talk about … well, different things,' she said with a giggle and smiled at him. She crossed, stretched and then re-crossed her legs. She glanced across at the cot. She was pleased to see baby Carl was sleeping peacefully.

Angel rubbed his chin. He thought it was time his questions were asked, answered and that he got the hell out of there. 'During your time at the Prophets', did you ever see Lady Cora Blessington?'

'Lady Cora Blessington? Sounds very posh. No. Who was she? Trevor asked me that?'

'A tall, blonde woman, in a long blue dress and trainers, frequently seen at the Prophets'.'

'No, Michael, I never saw anybody like that,' she said thoughtfully. Then she added, decisively, 'And being a blonde, believe me, I would have taken special notice of her.' She laughed.

'Did you ever hear either Mr or Mrs Prophet talk about Lady Blessington, refer to her, or to anybody like her? Her first name was Cora, by the way. Did they refer to anybody called Cora? Does that ring any bells?'

'No, and I'm sure I would have remembered someone with a name like that.'

'You never saw a letter or an envelope, took a message, saw a photograph or a card, with the name Lady Cora Blessington on it?'

'No, Michael. And I would have remembered a posh name like Lady Blessington.'

Angel squeezed an earlobe between finger and thumb. He really had expected Margaret Gaston to have met and seen the missing woman and thereby have filled in the many gaps. The annoying thing was that the person who knew the most about Lady Blessington was Alicia Prophet and she was dead. Lady B was just like the lady in the three card trick. Now you see her, now you don't. Some people had seen her, at a distance, fleetingly. Some people had never seen her at all. Angel had had some unusual cases over the years, but this was proving to be one of the most extraordinary.

'Anyway, who the hell was she?' Margaret Gaston said earnestly.

'I wish I knew. There's something else. There were some oranges in a plain white plastic bag found in the wheelie bin at Mr Prophet's house on Monday last, the day Mrs Prophet was murdered. They appear to have been dumped there. They were bought from a particular stall in Bromersley's open market. On that same day, Monday, at about two o'clock, you bought some oranges from the same stall. Were they the same ones?'

Her mouth dropped open.

'You've been checking up on me. No. I told you I didn't go near the Prophets' house on Monday. Monday is my day off. Anyway, why would I want to buy oranges and then throw them in the bin?'

'I don't know, Margaret. You tell me. Where are they now?'

'I've eaten them.'

Angel sighed. His eyes narrowed. 'When did you eat the last one?'

'Last night, while I was watching the telly.'

'What did you do with the peel?'

'The peel?'

'Yes.'

'Put it in the waste bin. Under the sink. In the kitchen.'

'Ah. Good. I'll have a look.'

'It's too late. I emptied it early this morning. It's been collected. I saw the dustbin lorry drive away.'

He pursed his lips and let out a long sigh.

She looked across at him.

'What's so special about orange peel? You didn't believe me. You were going to check up on me.'

'If you were the Archbishop of Canterbury I would have checked up on you.'

She rested her head in her hand and said, 'I suppose you have to.'

'Yes. I have to.'

There was a pause.

'Are you sure you wouldn't like a cup of tea or coffee?' she said. 'I've got a drop of sherry somewhere, if you'd rather,' she said mischievously. 'It would relax you, Michael. You're so tense. Are you like this at home? Are you married, Michael? What's your wife like?'

She wriggled up the settee, turned to face him, supporting her head with a hand and her arm on the armrest.

'Nothing for me to drink, thank you,' he said quickly. 'There's only one more thing,' he said.

'Are you hungry? I can do you a bacon sandwich.'

He shook his head quickly.

'The man who was living next door—'

'Number twenty. Yes. I heard he'd been murdered. Outside The Three Horseshoes. It's almost as if murder is following me about, isn't it?'

Angel thought about her last remark. If it was, she didn't seem at all phased by it. 'Did you know him?' he said.

'No. Saw him once come out of the lift. Looked a lonely, miserable little sod. Walked with his head down and his hands in his pockets. Didn't speak. Very quiet.'

'Did he have any visitors?'

'Don't think so. Never saw anybody. Never heard anything. Never even heard his telly through the wall. He must have heard mine.'

He rubbed his chin. 'Margaret. I'm going to have to ask you to vacate this flat tonight. It's for one night at least, although it could be for longer.'

Her face straightened. She sat bolt upright and stared at him. Her bottom lip quivered. 'You're not arresting me, are you?'

'Of course not,' he said quickly. 'It's for your safety, that's all.'

'I don't understand.'

'It's to do with your next door neighbour. We are expecting his place to be visited by somebody.'

'No,' she said. 'I don't want to go.'

He pulled his chin into his chest. 'It's really a matter of being extra careful, that's all. I'll make all the arrangements. Just assemble all you need for yourself and young Carl for, say, twenty-four hours. It's may not be as long as that. I'll get a WPC to come round and pick you up in an hour or so. She'll take you to our safe house. You'll be very comfortable. All mod cons. Telly, nice bathroom and everything. And absolutely safe.'

Her fingers went to her lips. She swivelled off the sofa. There was a flash of her long legs and white underwear. Angel tried to look away. He stood up.

She found the rabbit slippers and hurriedly pushed her feet into them. She shuddered, stood up and reached out for a cardigan hanging over a chair.

'I don't like it,' she said, stabbing an arm into a sleeve. 'Carl won't settle. He's never been away from here.'

Angel smiled at her. 'You'll be all right, just for a night.'

She wasn't happy.

'I don't want to go. Carl won't settle.'

'Just one night,' he said gently. 'It's for his and your safety.'

She nodded.

Angel glanced at an open door. 'Can I have a look around while I'm here?'

'Of course.'

He opened the door behind him. It was the kitchen. There were a few pots in a bowl in the sink, otherwise unremarkable. He came back into the room and looked at the next door. It was ajar.

'That's my bedroom,' she called out unnecessarily.

He didn't look back. He stepped forward a pace and pushed at the door. The hinges squeaked as it slowly swung open to reveal an unmade bed, a baby's cot with a mobile hanging over it and clothes strewn everywhere, both on the furniture, on the bed and on the floor. Then there was something that made Angel suck in a short intake of breath and which set his pulse racing. On the wall above the head of the bed was a picture. It was the painting of a young woman in a long blue frilly dress. She had blonde hair and a straw hat.

Margaret Gaston came forward. She saw that something had startled him.

'I haven't had chance to tidy round yet.'

He took a couple of steps up to the picture, pointed to it and said, 'Who is that?'

She looked up at it as if she'd never thought about it. 'I dunno. It was there when I took the flat. It's nobody. It's only a print.' She looked round the room at the explosion of clothes. 'I can tidy up. It won't take me long.'

Angel ran his hand through his hair.

'Do you mean it's always been there?'

'Since I've been here, it has. Do you want it, Michael? It's of no value, you know. It belongs by rights to Mother Reid, I suppose. If you want it, take it up with her.'

He sighed. He unhooked it off the tiny nail in the wall. It left a white mark on the dusty distempered wall. It weighed very little and was only about 20" by 30" on stout cardboard, framed by a thin wooden dowelling. He turned it over. There was a gold-coloured sticker on the back with black printing on it. '*1930s Lady of Leisure.* From the library of Joshua Pickering Galleries, 120-132 Argument Street, Farringdon, London. Stock No. 2239429.'

'What?' Angel bawled. He was surprised. He rubbed his chin thoughtfully.

Scrivens stood by the office door looking like a man who had won the lottery but lost the ticket.

'I said there's no such thing as 212 Huddersfield Road, sir. The numbers finish at 210. What's the point of that?'

Angel's lips tightened against his teeth. 'The point of *that*, Scrivens, is to validate Simon Spencer's existence dishonestly to the welfare state for free doctoring, free hospitals, subsidised dentistry and whatever other handouts he can get, without the exchequer and the judiciary being able to get back at him for taxes, fines and in this particular instance, fraud. And fraud *big time*.'

Scrivens raised his head.

'We have ourselves a very ambitious crook,' Angel said. 'And, I think, a murderer.'

'He may have murdered his partner in crime, Harry Harrison, sir?'

'It's getting to look that way. So hop off down to the Northern Bank. See the manager, Mr Thurrocks. Get the best possible description of Simon Spencer, you can. And get a photograph of him. Get a hundred prints of it with his description on it run off in time for this meeting at four o'clock, all right?'

Scrivens looked up as if a Roman candle had been fired up his trouser leg.

'Four o'clock, sir!' he cried, looking up at the wall clock. 'That only gives me an hour and a half.'

'Well, later than four would mean that the meeting would be pointless, wouldn't it? Come on, lad. Chop. Chop.'

The door closed.

Angel rubbed his chin. It wasn't looking good for Simon Spencer. He reached into his inside pocket and pulled out an envelope. There were some notes on the back of it. He ran down a list. He seemed satisfied that he had checked off all the points he needed to cover in preparation of the four o'clock briefing. He pulled out another envelope and began to check down that one. He found something. It was a telephone number. He picked up the phone and tapped it in.

'A1 Taxis,' a pert woman's voice replied.

'I want to speak to Maisie.'

There was a second's hesitation, then she drawled, 'Where do you wanna go?' She probably thought she was talking to a stranger who had discovered her name and was emboldened to speak familiarly to her after becoming shored up by the partaking of a few pints of some alcoholic beverage.

Angel squared up to phone. 'This is Detective Inspector Angel of Bromersley Police. I want to speak to the dispatcher who was on duty on Monday. One of your driver's, Albert Amersham, said it was a lady called Maisie. Is that you?'

The woman's voice changed. She suddenly became vital. 'Oh. Yes. Yes, sir. I'm Maisie Evans. I was on duty on Monday from ten until six. Yes. What can I do for you, sir?'

'This is a police inquiry, young lady. Someone booked a taxi from Wells Street Baths to The Beeches, 22 Creesforth Road. Your driver picked up the fare from the baths just before two o'clock. What can you tell me about the booking? Presumably it was phoned in. Who phoned it in and where did they phone from?'

'It should be in the book. Please hold on, I'll look it up.'

She wasn't long. 'It was me, sir, and I remember it now, because the caller said she was Lady Blessington or some such. She spelled the ruddy name out for me. We don't get many "Ladies" ringing in for taxis here, I can tell you. She was very snooty. She rang in herself. One of those strained, clever dick voices straight from *Panorama*. At first, I thought it was somebody fooling around. I logged it at 1.40 p.m. I radioed it straight through to number eight, that was Bert Amersham. We had a bit of a laugh about the ladyship bit. I've no idea where she phoned in from. We don't keep no records of that.'

'Thank you, Maisie,' he said and replaced the phone.

It wasn't much help, but it did at least confirm the fact that a taxi had been summoned to Wells Street Baths at that particular time, and by the mysterious Lady Blessington. Angel liked to build his cases on facts.

There was a knock at the door. It was Ahmed. He was carrying a sheet of paper.

'What is it, lad?' Angel grumbled. 'Don't you think I've got enough on my plate?

'Only take a second, sir. You wanted me to make a thorough search of the NPC. See if there were any female villains on the loose. Done that. There's only one, who has been released recently, and who has been known to carry a handgun. She's Lily Frodsham, 37, blonde. I've made inquiries and she's in a hospital in Manchester.'

Angel sighed.

'Thanks, Ahmed. It's not her. I know of her. That's light-fingered Lil. Confidence trickster par excellence. Marries anything with money. Fills her bank account, her handbag, her boots and her pockets and then disappears. She's in hospital because one of her husbands had caught up with her and tried to murder her with a swimming pool rake.'

Lines of bewilderment appeared on Ahmed's forehead. He dared not ask Angel for more details.

Gawber's face appeared beyond Ahmed's.

'You wanted me, sir?' He asked.

Angel put up a finger. 'Yes. Come in, Ron.'

Ahmed quietly closed the door.

Angel had been eagerly waiting to see him. He reached down the side of his desk and pulled up the print of the *1930s Lady of Leisure* and rested it on the desk. He explained where he had found it and said: 'This print appears to be a near representation of the mysterious Lady Blessington.'

Both Ahmed and Gawber stared at it open-mouthed.

'How is it possible that Margaret Gaston has been living with the picture for nearly two years and yet knows nothing about the woman in real life?' Angel said.

'But it's not a recent painting of the woman?' Gawber said. 'It can't be.'

'It isn't. It's just a close representation of her. The dress, the hat and the hairdo are the same as in the photo. You can't see her feet. I guess the model would have worn elegant sandals, fashion of the day. The lack of lines on the face suggests she's young … under twenty-five, whereas we are told by all the witnesses of Lady B that she is forty to sixty.'

'I don't understand, sir,' Gawber said.

'Nor do I,' Ahmed added.

'Join the club,' Angel said. 'What's a picture of Lady blooming Blessington doing in Margaret Gaston's bedroom?'

Gawber and Ahmed looked puzzled.
'It's a coincidence, sir,' Gawber said. 'It's got to be.'
Ahmed nodded agreement.
Angel pursed his lips and shook his head.
Gawber remembered: Angel didn't believe in coincidences.

CHAPTER NINE

There were about twenty uniformed and plainclothes women and men in the briefing room, chattering away to each other and sipping drinks out of paper cups. Each was in possession of an A4 computer-printed photo and description of Simon Spencer which Scrivens had handed to them on their arrival.

Angel arrived on the dot of 1600 hours carrying the print of the *1930s Lady of Leisure*. Ahmed followed him in and closed the door. Gawber came up to him, they exchanged a few words and then Angel stepped up onto the dais.

All talking stopped and everybody looked attentively at him.

'Two things I want to talk about briefly. Firstly, in connection with the Alicia Prophet murder.'

He held up the framed print. 'I am looking for a woman who looks something like this. We have witnesses who say that such a woman murdered the blind Mrs Prophet on Monday afternoon. Now I have been in touch with the publishers of this print. They sold many thousands of them when this sort of thing was popular in the sixties. They stopped selling this particular one in 1966. They don't know who the original artist was, and the model is almost certainly dead by now having enjoyed a perfectly normal, boring life. The landlady at the flat where it was found said that it must have been left by a tenant many years ago. She can't recall how long since. Nevertheless, I am given to understand that this is a fair representation of what the wanted woman actually looks like. The real life woman, I am told is older … between 40 and 60 years, and calls herself Lady Blessington, but our enquiries indicate that that name is false. But she is a murderer and confidence trickster of a very high calibre; therefore, be on the lookout for her, she may strike again. Obviously, if you see anybody who looks like this let me know.'

He stopped, looked up the room and said: 'Any questions on that?'

A voice at the front said: 'If that's a picture of what the murderer looks like now sir, how is it that … it was painted all that time ago?'

Angel licked his bottom lip. 'I don't know, John. I don't know,' he said quickly. 'Just go along with me on this for the time being, will you?'

He observed a few murmurs of confusion and incredulity from several officers. 'I can't explain it,' he added. 'I only came across the thing today. I hope to clarify the matter in due course.'

He handed the print to Ahmed and indicated that he should stick it on the wall behind him.

A voice called out from the back. 'I thought the murderer was thought to be Reynard, sir. Orange peel being found around the body and that.… Is there any mileage in that theory at all?'

'At the moment, nothing is set in stone. Please keep your mind on finding Lady Blessington or whatever her real name is.'

There were a few more murmurs.

'Can we move on?' he said. 'Now apropos the murder yesterday of Harry Harrison, aka Harry Henderson, inquiries have led us to believe that his murderer was possibly his partner in crime Simon Spencer, until recently an apparently respectable teller at the Northern Bank. The two of them worked a brazen fraud against the Smith family some of whom tragically perished in the tsunami in 2004. The two men connived to extract two million pounds in small sums from the Smith's bank account. Spencer was, of course, the inside man … fiddling with the post and matters of security within the bank, while Harrison was forging away, purporting to be Simon Smith and calling in the bank only when the manager was away, or at lunch, or as directed by Spencer. Having drained the Smith's account, it looks as if Harrison then beetled off and hid the money in an attempt to trick Spencer out of his share. There is no evidence to show that Spencer had ever been to Harrison's flat, so we are inclined to believe that he didn't know his last address. This supposition is supported by the fact that he was murdered outside in a pub car-park, which is only round the corner from the victim's flat. We therefore assume that they quarrelled and Spencer stabbed him to death and dumped him in the skip. Last night I arranged that the *Examiner* should report the case in this morning's edition and print Harrison's address, Flat 20, on the top-floor in the block of flats at the top of Mansion Hill. Some of you may have seen it in the paper. So tonight, I believe, will be the first night Spencer will have become aware of his associate's address and likely hiding place. And I hope and believe that he will be on his tippy-toes anxious to get into the flat and search it for the money, which we have, of course, already found and removed. There are only two attic flats on the top-floor. I have arranged for the other tenant and her baby, living in Number 19, to be accommodated in the safe house, and the landlady has agreed not to re-let Harrison's flat, so that tonight the entire top floor will be unoccupied and in darkness. Now I think that Spencer will be desperate and dangerous. He will be armed, possibly with a blade, so we need to be armed, alert and efficient.'

Looks were exchanged among the officers.

He continued. 'There are two entrances to the flat. There's the front door that leads straight from the pavement on Mansion Hill into the ground floor. It is always locked and can only be opened by tapping in the combination, known only to the landlady and the tenants. And there is a side door which leads through to a small backyard where the waste bins are located. The ground floor consists of four flats, two utility rooms, the lift and the stairs. The side door is usually locked by two heavy bolts. I have arranged for the bolts to be removed, so that the door cannot be locked, and so that Spencer should not have too much difficulty in gaining access. Nevertheless, this might be an all-night vigil. I want the white surveillance van to be parked on Rotherham Road. There's a position there that would give us sight of both doors. I will be in there with DS Gawber. I have briefed two teams, each of two armed men, who will be joining us from the FSU at Wakefield. They will be in unmarked cars and parked well out of sight somewhere in Chapel Street or off Rotherham Road. They will be hidden from nosey parkers, but close enough to be brought in at short notice. This operation will start at 2100 hours. Everybody not directly involved, particularly drivers of marked cars, be aware to keep away from the area until dawn tomorrow, please. Any questions?'

A voice called out from the back.

'Have you some specific intelligence that Spencer will show, sir?'

Angel frowned. 'No. He may not show, of course. But two million pounds is a powerfully strong reason why he probably will.'

'Is Spencer known to have any criminal associates, sir?' another voice called out.

'No. You mean … will he come alone? I believe this fraud was virtually his maiden job. He's hardly had the opportunity to become a member of a gang.'

The questioner seemed satisfied.

'Anything else?' Angel said. He looked round. 'Right. Thank you very much everybody. Just one more thing, I'd like to emphasize. This man has murdered in one of the most savage ways I know. Sticking a knife into a man, pulling it out covered in blood and then sticking it back into him, several times. He's desperate. He connived at extricating two million pounds out of a bank account. He had given up his job and was planning how to spend it. It was almost in his grasp. Then suddenly his partner crossed him. His crooked plan began to fall apart. I believe he tried to scare Harrison into telling him where he'd hidden the money. In the quarrel, he stabbed him several times before he was dead. He's a nasty piece of work, so don't let's take any chances with him. Let's get him off the streets.'

It was 10.30 p.m. and the moon was high. A pleasant summer breeze blew. It hadn't rained for a good forty-eight hours and dry warm weather was forecast.

Angel and Gawber arrived in the white observation van and parked it at the side of the road in a line of cars on Rotherham Road. They had an excellent view of the side door of Mansion Hill flats with the wheelie bins clustered in an area contained by a low brick wall broken by a gateway, the gate having long since been lifted off its hinges and discarded. The van, being at right angles to the street known as Mansion Hill, allowed the occupants a good view of a narrow strip of the front door, so that they were in a perfect position to be able to observe all access to and from the building. Their only light source was to be the moon, which tonight was adequate for the job they had to do.

Angel had settled himself on a stool in the back of the van. He was setting up the night binoculars on a table tripod on the bench fitted under the one-way window that faced the flats.

Gawber had unpacked the video camera, fitted it with a night lens and was unravelling the cable to plug it into the power socket on the bench.

'Got a brand new tape, sir. Lasts ninety minutes,' he said chirpily.

Angel only grunted in reply. He felt down into his suit coat pocket and pulled out a Glock hand pistol. It was the

G 17, the standard model, only 7" long, that just fitted into the pocket. He pressed the catch on the stock, allowing the magazine to be ejected. It dropped into his hand. He checked the magazine spring by pressing the top round with his forefinger. It gave hardly at all, indicating that the first round was in the correct position and that the magazine was full. It held seventeen deadly 9mm bullets. It made a solid click as he pushed the magazine back into the stock. He stuffed the gun back into his pocket. Then he switched on the RT and reached out for the microphone.

'Traveller One to Romeo Lima One. Are you all set?'

'Yes, sir? We're in position, up a ginnel off Chapel Street.'

'Everything all right?'

'There's an old woman in a nightdress ... keeps peering out of a back upstairs window at us, sir. I think she thinks we're a couple of peeping Toms.'

Angel pulled a face. 'I don't want anything to cause a disturbance or divert your attention. Either speak to her and settle her down now or move to another position.'

'We'll move, sir.'

'Call in when you're in position.'

'Right, sir.'

'Traveller One to Romeo Lima Two. Are you all set?'

'Yes, sir. We're in a line of parked empty cars about 300 yards away on Chapel Street. Nobody is around. Nobody seems to have noticed us. We can be at the target house in about thirty seconds.'

Angel fished around into a bag under the table and pulled out a flask that Mary had prepared for him and poured a drink into a little china cup. He sipped it and made an appreciative noise.

A few minutes passed, then a voice on the RT said: 'Romeo Lima Two to Traveller One.'

'Right, come in, lad.'

'We're up the next ginnel and a bit nearer, sir. Just round the corner, in fact.'

'OK. Keep the line open. Report any sighting of a solitary man about thirty years of age … he might be on foot … or in a car or even on a bicycle, I suppose.'

'Right, sir.'

Angel turned to Gawber. 'The last time I was out on a night obbo was that murder on Sycamore Grove. Remember?'

'I do. Your missus was away because her mother was ill and you made yourself some beetroot sandwiches. Ahmed felt sorry for you and offered you some strange concoction that his mother had made him.'

They both smiled.

A voice through the RT said, 'If anybody's hungry I've got some roast beef.'

'Thank you, lad,' Angel said with a grin.

Angel watched the fluorescent clock on the bench front show midnight and shortly afterwards heard St Mary's Church clock strike twelve. The moon was shining quite brightly. There were no clouds, so it was about as dark as it was going to get. Some time passed in silence, then suddenly there was a voice through the RT.

'Romeo Lima Two to Traveller One.'

There was something urgent about the way the man spoke. Angel felt his heart bounce. 'Yes, Romeo Lima Two?'

'A big car has just passed us, sir. Very slowly.'

Angel's pulse beat loudly in his ears.

'I think it's black,' Romeo Lima Two continued. 'Moving slowly … like a hearse … as if it's surveying the area. It's turning left.'

Angel breathed out a cool sigh.

'Just the driver in it?'

'Couldn't see, sir. It's got the lines of a big Mercedes. It's coming your way.'

The vehicle suddenly glided alongside the observation van and stopped. The near side was only eight feet away.

Angel heard Gawber gasp excitedly as he gripped the handle of the video camera tightly and traversed the full length of the Mercedes.

Angel could feel and hear the vibration of the car engine. It cut off his view of the flat. All he could see were black windows and black bodywork.

The car hovered for a few seconds.

He sniffed and peered harder through the binoculars. 'It's a big, expensive piece of transport for one bank clerk,' he whispered.

He sat glued to the binoculars trying to catch sight of the driver.

After a few seconds the car rolled silently away down Rotherham Road.

Angel eased back from the binoculars and rubbed his chin.

'Did you get the index number?'

'Yes, sir. I'll ring it through.'

'Do it now.'

'I hope we've not frightened him off,' Gawber said, reaching out for his mobile.

'Naw,' Angel said, wiping his face with his handkerchief. 'He'll be back. He's very nervous. Very careful.'

He reached out for the microphone. 'Romeo Lima One and Two. I'm pretty sure that this is the customer we're expecting. Keep your heads down. He'll be back soon and might come checking round all parked cars. Be very careful.'

Two minutes later, Gawber turned away from his mobile phone and said, 'The car is registered to a Doctor Shannon in Cambridge.'

Angel nodded. 'It'll be twinned. I don't like this, Ron. This isn't Spencer. It bears all the signs of a heavy gang.' He felt a tingle through his chest. The hairs on the back of his neck stood up.

Five minutes later, the big black car arrived back on Rotherham Road. The car taxied up to Mansion Hill flats like a jumbo jet fitted with a silencer. It stopped gently only feet away.

Angel felt his heart pounding again.

Gawber reached out for the video camera and pulled the trigger.

All four doors opened and a man got out of each door. The two nearest men were giants. They looked like the offspring of a steam train and a pipe-works. They were armed with short, light pieces carried at thigh height. They looked like old Sten guns. The other two were merely tall and wiry and carried something in their right hands. They were all dressed in dark coloured T-shirts, jeans and black jockey caps with the neb facing backwards. They made straight across the road to the side door of the flats.

The car glided silently away.

Angel's breathing was heavy. He knew that plan A was down the pan, and anybody with half a brain could pull the chain. This was a far bigger operation than he had expected. He reached out for the mike. 'Traveller One to Romeo Lima One.'

'Romeo Lima One here, sir.'

'Go quickly to the station, to Traffic, and get a magnetic tracer. Make sure it has a new battery and bring it back to me, smartly.'

'On our way, sir.'

Gawber said: 'The four men have found the back door and they've gone inside, sir.'

Angel peered through the binoculars. The street was quiet and deserted.

He grabbed the microphone again. 'Traveller One to Romeo Lima Two.'

'Romeo Lima Two here, sir.'

'Run around the area, *once* only, and see if you can see where the Mercedes has toddled off to. It won't be far away. Don't go down the same street twice. You understand? The driver might just be sauntering round while the others are taking the flat to pieces and awaiting a signal from them, or it may be just parked up somewhere handy. But be *careful*. Don't let them realize what you are doing. Drive away noisily if you think they suspect.'

'Right, sir.'

He returned to the binoculars. Nothing moved. In the moonlight, he could just make out the lids of the wheelie bins and the glass panel in the door. There was a long, long silence. Five minutes. Ten minutes. He listened for the slightest sound. Nothing moved. There was zilch. Zero. Just the thumping of his pulse. It was so quiet, still and in moonlight ... as if it was the final day on earth.

Then the RT crackled. 'Romeo Lima Two here, sir. Can't see the car anywhere, sir. Been all round.'

'All right. Get back in position.'

'Right, sir.'

Angel returned to the window and peered upwards. 'I wonder how they're getting along up there?'

'They must have been in the flat about twelve minutes,' Gawber added.

Angel brushed a sweaty hand through his hair. That was a long time in this business. It was much longer than he expected them to be. They must have felt pretty confident to have taken so long. He leaned forward to the microphone. 'Traveller One to Romeo Lima One. How much longer are you going to be?'

'On our way, sir.'

'Yeah, but what's your ETA?'

'About two minutes, sir.'

'Make it one. Come in quietly. I'll meet you on foot on Chapel Street ... at the first ginnel. Has that thing got a fresh battery?'

'Fitted while we waited, sir.'

'See you in a minute.'

'Right, sir.'

Gawber stared towards Angel. He couldn't believe it. 'You're not going out, sir, on your own?' he breathed.

Angel stood up. 'The Merc's not back yet. I'm hoping I've time.'

'You can't go out, sir. You'll be *seen*!'

'Only if anybody's looking,' he said and he opened the door and slipped out on the pavement.

'But, sir,' Gawber protested.

He could have saved his breath.

It was bright. There was a lot of moon and no sign of a cloud.

Angel knew that there was no possible chance of not being seen walking down the street if anybody had been watching, so he walked boldly along to the corner of Rotherham Road. It was only a few yards onto Chapel Street, and only a few more to where Romeo Lima One had been hiding. Seconds later, the car arrived. Seeing him, it slowed. The front nearside window was down. He held out his hand and was handed a metal disc about the diameter of a truncheon and as thick as a bullet. 'Thanks, lad.'

'Good luck, sir.'

He pushed it into his pocket and retraced his steps boldly to the observation van. There was still no sign of any members of the gang or of the Mercedes. He sighed with relief as he stepped noiselessly into the van and closed the door.

There was a crackle from the RT. 'The Merc's back, sir. It's coming your way.'

'Right. Ta,' Angel replied.

Almost immediately, the big black car pulled across the window of the observation van.

Angel silently slid the door of the van open, and made his way along the pavement and onto the road, crouching down at the rear of the observation van.

At the same time, four men dashed out of the flats across the road to the Mercedes; all four doors were opened, a man entered through each door, and then they closed them almost as one, like an army drill.

That was Angel's cue. He knew he had less than a second. He darted from behind the observation van, crouched down and placed the magnetic tracking device under the nearside wheel arch of the Mercedes, and at the same time received a face full of exhaust fumes. He fell backwards onto his rear as the Mercedes sped away along Rotherham Road.

CHAPTER TEN

Angel stood the team down, returned to the station, handed his gun into the desk sergeant to be held in safe-custody until the armourer came on duty, went home and was in bed for 2 a.m. He had almost six hours sleep, an easy breakfast with Mary and was back in the office as fresh as a home-baked bap by 8.28 a.m.

As he walked into the office, his phone was ringing. He raised his eyebrows as he leaned over the desk and picked up the handset. It was Harker.

'I want you, lad,' the superintendent bawled. 'Come up here, smartish.' Then there was a loud click; the line went dead. Angel replaced the phone and wrinkled up his nose. He wondered what sort of a flea had got in Harker's vest that early in the morning. He sounded threatening and was obviously in a bad mood.

'What do you think you are playing at?' Harker roared as he entered the office.

Angel stared back at him, sitting behind his desk looking like an orang-utan with toothache. The vein on his left temple throbbed at the beat of *The Ritual Fire Dance.*

Angel sighed, closed the door and came up to the desk. 'What's the matter, sir?'

'I understand that you've put a young lass and her child in the safe house up at Beechfield Walk.'

'Yes, sir. Well, it was the only safe thing to do. She is the mother of an eighteen-month child and—'

'A one-parent family, eh?'

'I believe so, sir.'

'Oh I see. You're fancying a bit of young easy skirt, is that it?'

Angel's jaw tightened. 'No, sir. I was setting a trap to catch the man whom I think is Harrison's murderer, a Simon Spencer,' he said. 'This young woman might have been in the line of fire. It was for one night only. She can return back to her flat this morning.'

'You realize that it has taken WPC Baverstock off her regular duties to play nursemaid to this lass and her offspring, don't you?'

'Well, I knew that somebody would have to—'

'And did you think of the cost? And the shortage of officers?' He suddenly stopped. 'What trap? Who did you catch?'

'I didn't catch anybody, sir. But I enticed a bigger fish than—'

'A bigger fish? Who? *Who*?' he yelled excitedly.

'I don't know, sir,' Angel said trying to control his temper. 'It was obviously an organized gang of four men and a driver, armed to the teeth. We couldn't possibly have taken them on. They were tooled up and ready for a fight. A commitment there and then would have resulted in a blood bath.'

Harker threw up his arms.

'Well, where are they? *Who* are they? You talk grand, but you've let them get away.'

Angel sighed.

'We had to remain concealed, sir, but I put a tracking device on their car. I was about to phone DS Mallin in Traffic to find out where their car is now.'

Harker's face changed. The tirade stopped.

'Hmmm,' he grunted thoughtfully. It seemed to please him. He sat down and rubbed his chin. Then he reached out for the phone and tapped in a number.

Standing in front of the desk, Angel could hear a distorted reply through the earpiece.

'Mallin? You're monitoring a tracking device for DI Angel. Has it come to rest yet, and if so, whereabouts?' Harker said.

There was more distorted chat from the earpiece.

'Right,' he snapped and dropped the phone back in its cradle. He sniffed. 'As I thought. It's from some green-belt land just off the motorway on the road to Huddersfield. It'll have been discovered and thrown away. If the gang's as professional as you said it was, it would be wary of tricks like that.'

Angel pursed his lips. Maybe. Maybe not. Anyway, in his experience, when tracking devices had been found by crooks, they used to transfer them to a different vehicle. It amused them to think of the police tailing some innocent lorry or bus driver pointlessly around the countryside.

'I want you to get that girl and her infant out of Beechfield Walk. Let WPC Baverstock get back to her duties, and you get back to those two unsolved murder cases. You've got *plenty* on your plate, lad.'

'Yes, sir.'

Angel drove the BMW northwards on the road towards Huddersfield. Sitting next to him was Gawber who was looking at a laptop monitor showing the map and flashing co-ordinates indicating the whereabouts of the Mercedes. The flashing arrow on the screen showed that they needed to move west and north, so Angel left the main road and was directed to travel up a narrow unmade road, like a cart-track, almost parallel to the motorway. It was built up on the left like the banking on a railway track. Both sides were overhung with long grass interspersed with nettles and rosebay willow-herb.

The intensity of the signal showed that they were dead on course for the tracking device.

Angel frowned as the car rocked and splashed through a puddle on the uneven track. 'Up here?' he said.

'We are very close, sir.'

'Can't see anything but grass and weeds.'

Angel suddenly had to take a bend round to the right and came onto an open piece of rough ground hardened with clinker from burnt-out coal fires and big enough for a vehicle to turn round. He pulled up in front of a sign. It read: 'KEEP OUT. Private Property. Employees Grock's Rhubarb Limited only'.

He read the sign and rubbed his chin.

Behind the sign was a large padlocked gate and beyond that a large spread of low buildings, thirty or more, built close together, in total extending to the size of a football pitch. They appeared to be mainly constructed from corrugated metal sheets and timber, arched like miniature airplane hangars, eight feet tall at the highest point. They had been heavily repaired and patched with all kinds of oddments, sides of packing cases, tea chests, bed heads, tin advertising signs for Mazawattee Tea, Senior Service and Zubes. The structures were roughly weatherproofed with brattice-cloth and heavily daubed with a mixture of tar and creosote. There were no windows and each building had large double doors with a padlock securing it. The place seemed deserted.

Angel looked around and pursed his lips.

'Ah. They're rhubarb forcing sheds,' he said.

'It doesn't seem the likely HQ for an armed gang, sir?'

He nodded in agreement and looked across at the monitor. It showed that they were dead on target. 'This thing is accurate to about forty yards. That car must be in one of these sheds, Ron.'

'Which one?'

Angel shrugged and got out of the car. 'There's nobody about. Let's take a look round.'

The sign indicated that they had reached a dead end so far as vehicles were concerned. Angel looked through the wooden spars of the gate. There was no sign of anybody. As he turned away, he spotted a trodden pathway between the fence and a hawthorn hedge.

'Let's see where this leads,' Angel said.

They made their way along it for about twenty yards to another hedge with a stile through it. They looked over the stile into a small clearing with an imposing country house ahead, and a barn on the right of it. There was a formal drive up to the house from the left. Angel reckoned that the drive to the house and barn must be accessible from somewhere on the main Bromersley to Huddersfield Road.

Gawber made to climb the stile.

Angel suddenly grabbed the sleeve of his coat. 'Hang on, Ron,' he whispered urgently and pulled him behind the hawthorn hedge. 'There's somebody coming out of the house.'

Sure enough, from behind the hedge they saw a huge man in a black T-shirt, jeans, trainers and the distinctive jockey cap worn the wrong way. He appeared on the front doorstep of the house. He looked round, then went back in and returned with a slim, young man in a suit. The young man's head was hanging down, his hands appeared to be tied behind his back. The big man frog-marched him down the steps and across the drive to the barn. The big door was open and fastened back. They went inside.

Angel's pulse began to race.

Gawber and Angel exchanged glances.

'There's one of them,' Angel whispered. 'Did you recognize the other man?'

Gawber shook his head.

This was an important discovery. It looked as if they had found the headquarters of the armed gang who had raided Harrison's flat the previous night. This journey was proving very profitable.

Angel reached into his pocket for his mobile and dialled a number.

'Keep an eye out. I'll get some back-up.'

Eventually he got through to his old friend Waldo White. He was the Detective Inspector in charge of the Firearms Support Unit at Wakefield. After they had exchanged pleasantries, Angel put him in the picture and told him their location.

'There are four men, at least, in the gang, and they are all armed. A head-on confrontation would result in the exchange of fire. I want to avoid that.'

Angel explained that they were up the cart track and at the entrance to Grock's Rhubarb forcing sheds. They agreed to meet there.

White said: 'We'll come straightaway.'

Angel closed down his phone and was about to drop it into his pocket when they suddenly heard a loud and disagreeable voice just behind them say, 'What are you doing here? Don't you know you're trespassing?'

They looked round to see a tall, slim man with heavy five o'clock shadow. He was pointing a hand gun at them.

Angel could see it was a Walther PPK/S. Deadly and accurate from twenty or thirty feet. Angel's and Gawber's hearts started thumping.

Angel's recognized him as another member of the gang. His heart leapt. For a moment, he couldn't speak. He had a natural aversion to firearms … especially when they were in the hands of somebody else and were being pointed directly at him. He still had the mobile in his hand. He opened his fingers and deliberately let it fall to the ground. It landed silently in a tuft of grass. He hoped that that it might be discovered by Waldo White and that he might realize he had been there.

'Put your hands up,' the man growled. 'I've had a good look at your car, so I know you're coppers.'

'What's the gun for?' Angel said.

'Shut up, put your hands up, face your front and get over that stile.'

'What do you want with us?' Angel said.

'Shut up,' the man said.

He marched them across the field to the barn.

Angel's mind was working overtime. They were in a fix and he couldn't see a way out.

The man with the gun directed them into the barn. The young man in a suit whom they had seen being frog-marched from the house, was being tied up by the big man. His hands were being secured behind him in a standing position to a sturdy pole, one of four, which supported the barn roof. The young man stared across at Angel and Gawber with glazed eyes but without any emotion. His pasty face had grey patches under the eyes. Angel knew he had been drugged. He thought he had seen a photograph of him recently, but he couldn't quite place him.

The thug finished tying the man up and turned round as he heard their footsteps. His eyes opened up like bus headlights being switched on. His jaw dropped. 'Who are they?' he growled.

'Coppers. Snooping around.'

'Coppers!' he shrieked. He raised the Sten gun. His hands were shaking. 'What you brought them here for? What are *we* going to do with them?'

'I don't know,' replied the slim man angrily. He pointed a thumb towards the open door. 'Tell Eddie. Tell him we've got company.'

The big man rushed out of the barn, shaking his head and muttering expletives.

'What do you want with us,' Angel said to the man with the Walther.

'Shut up,' the man said thrusting the gun into his Angel's stomach. 'Don't you understand plain English?'

Angel's faced reddened. He could hear his pulse banging away in his ears.

Seconds later, three men and a young woman appeared at the open barn door; they stared open-mouthed at Angel and Gawber. The two heavies with menacing expressions, their stock-in-trade, carried old Sten guns and pointed them at them. The third, an older man with a face as hard as a life sentence, waved another Walther in their general direction.

Angel wished he was anywhere but there. His eyes darted round their sockets. He was seeking and searching for any opportunity to get away.

The older man with the Walther stared angrily at the younger man and said: 'What you got here, kid? Ox said they are coppers. Are you completely off your trolley?'

'They were snooping round. I had no choice, Eddie,' he said.

Angel clocked the name 'Eddie.' He remembered the prison photograph of the man in the Police Review. It took only a second to work out that it was the Glazer gang, on the run. It was Eddie 'The Cat' Glazer, his wife, Oona, and his younger brother, Tony. He didn't know the two big men, though he had just heard one of them referred to as 'Ox'.

The younger brother, Tony, continued: 'Their car was parked at the farm gate. They were snooping through the hedge at the house.' There was a whine in his voice. He was clearly afraid of his elder brother.

'Have you searched them?' Eddie snapped.

'How could I? I was on my own. He dropped this,' Tony said, handing him the mobile which Angel had discarded in the long grass. 'Thought I hadn't noticed.'

Angel bit his bottom lip. He didn't know that Tony Glazer had found it.

Eddie took it, glanced at it then at Angel.

'Clever copper. I don't want it,' he snarled. 'No use to me!' he added and threw it angrily into the straw at the back of the barn and glared suspiciously at Angel and then at Gawber.

Angel sighed inwardly. He didn't like the situation one bit. He hoped that when Waldo White discovered that they weren't at the rendezvous, that he would hunt around for them, find them and that that would be sooner rather than later.

'Well bloody well search them then now,' Eddie yelled. 'They might be armed, or wired up and telling the world where we are.'

Tony stuck the Walther into his waistband and began to pat Angel down.

Eddie glared at Ox and waved the gun in the direction of Gawber. Ox dropped the Sten so that it hung loose on the strap from his shoulder. He turned Gawber round and began to pat him down.

Tony took out Angel's wallet, badge and ID card. He passed them to Eddie, who angrily snatched them from him.

Eddie glared at Angel and said, 'How did you find us, copper?'

'Fancied rhubarb pie for tea, but there was nobody about, Mr *Glazer*. You know, you'll never sell rhubarb if you keep the place shut.'

Eddie glared at him as he fingered roughly through his wallet and ID.

The girl Oona was terrified. Her hands were shaking. Her face was redder than a monkey's backside. She grabbed Eddie by the arm. 'He knows who you are! What are we going to do?' she wailed. '*What are we going to do*?'

'Shut up. And get off,' he said, pushing her away. 'Detective Inspector Angel,' he said scornfully, reading from the ID. He threw the wallet, badge and ID angrily into the straw behind them. 'Well, well, well. You're the smart-arse inspector looking for the murderer of Harry Harrison, aren't you?'

Angel looked at him.

Eddie pointed to the man tied up with his head bowed. 'Well there's your murderer. Spencer's his name. I've done your job for you.'

Angel looked across at the man tied to the post. His eyes were closed. He seemed to be asleep. He *hoped* he was asleep. Angel had to agree, the man did look a bit like the photograph of Spencer, which Thurrocks, the bank manager had supplied.

'He and Harrison worked a scam across a rich punter at the Northern Bank called Smith,' Eddie continued. 'Harrison got greedy and tried to put one across Spencer. He got wise to it and threatened to cut him up if he didn't tell him where he'd hidden the money. Harrison refused. Spencer went in a bit too heavy, and Harry died before he told him where he'd hidden it. That's what *he* said, anyway. Stabbed him five times.'

Angel pursed his lips. He wondered why Eddie Glazer should be volunteering information so freely. Hard nuts like him never gave information away for nothing.

Ox handed Gawber's wallet, badge and ID to Eddie. He rummaged through the wallet, read the ID and said, 'Just another rubbish copper. A bleeding sergeant!'

He angrily threw the wallet, badge and ID into the straw.

Angel's lips tightened back against his teeth. 'What have you done to him?' he said, nodding towards Spencer. 'He doesn't look well.'

'He'll be all right,' Eddie said. 'Just getting over a hangover, that's all,' he added with a grin.

Angel turned away. Eddie's breath smelled. Angel thought he should see a dentist urgently for a scale and polish.

'What's he doing tied up?' Angel said.

'He's a murderer. I've told you.'

Angel pursed his lips.

'Does anybody else know you're here, copper?'

The barrel of the Walther was getting ever nearer; Glazer was waving the gun about like a kid with a flag at a coronation. Angel's mind was wonderfully concentrated. He knew he could be dead in a second.

'Of course,' he said evenly. That was the only reply he could have given. Those few words might help save their lives.

Eddie snarled. It wasn't the reply he wanted to hear.

'I don't believe you,' he said. 'You're just a frigging liar. Say anything to save your skin.'

'Why did I have a phone in my hand then, Eddie? Did you think I was ordering custard?' Angel said.

'Custard?' Eddie bawled. 'What yer frigging on about?'

'To go with the rhubarb,' Angel said.

Eddie Glazer's face tightened. He was thinking about what to say.

Ox sighed loudly and growled. 'Come on. What we going to do with them, Eddie,' he said gruffly.

'Yeah. We're wasting time. We need to get way from here, *now*,' Tony yelled.

'I'm for clearing out,' Ox growled.

'We gotta get away from here, Eddie,' Oona wailed and grabbed his arm.

'Shut up or I'll belt you one,' he snarled and pulled away from her. He pulled a face like a man who remembered the taste of prison hootch. He ran a hand through his greasy hair and swivelled angrily round to face them. 'All right!' he bawled. 'All right!' Then he added quickly: 'Oona bring the Merc round to the front. Ox and Kenny, tie these coppers up. Make it good. Tony, stay with them. Keep your gun on them. Then come back to the house. We'll take just the money and the ammo. Leave everything else. Right, now, all of you, *move it*!'

Eddie and Oona ran out of the barn.

Tony stood by the open door pointing his gun straight ahead at Angel and Gawber. Ox snatched some pieces of rope from a few lengths hanging from a big hook screwed onto the barn side, no doubt used to tether animals in the past. He tossed a length over to Kenny and they both began tying the wrists of Angel and Gawber around the wooden support posts. They did it roughly, quickly, silently and efficiently. Then they ran out of the barn towards the house. Tony stuffed the gun in his waist band and dashed over to Angel. He went round the back of the post, looked at the fastening and then checked the tightness. He moved over to the next post and checked Gawber, then Spencer in the same way. He seemed satisfied. He took one quick look round, then dashed out of the barn, unhooked the door and closed it.

There was easily enough light from under the door for Angel to see Gawber tied to a post about ten feet away and Spencer, still with his head dropped, another ten feet further away in a line down the middle of the barn.

'What now?' Gawber said.

'Can you get out of it, Ron?' Angel said.

They wriggled and struggled briefly, their faces perspiring and getting redder and redder, but their captors had made a secure job.

'No, sir. What do think will happen now?'

'If Waldo White hasn't got lost, the FSU should be here anytime.'

A car door slammed.

'Is that them?'

'Too quiet. It'll be Glazer's car, the Mercedes.'

'They're going to get away, sir.'

Angel knew he was right, and he was not in a position to stop them. It would be quite dreadful allowing that armed mob back on the streets again. But he was thankful that the gang had left them unharmed. It was really not Glazer's style. Angel had expected to be shot or tortured or knocked about. As it was, he hoped White would find them, let it not be long.

The barn door suddenly opened. It was Eddie Glazer. He had a wild expression on his face, which was also shining with perspiration. He was carrying what looked like a glass bottle. It had a small trail of cloth hanging out of the neck.

'I'll teach you coppers not to come looking for me,' he yelled, his eyes flashing. 'But you'll never do it again!'

Angel could now see what he had in his hand.

It was a Molotov cocktail: a bottle of petrol with a soaked wick hanging out of it. Ignited and thrown into the barn amid all the dry straw, it would create a colossal blaze.

Angel's heart sank.

Glazer plunged his hand in his pocket. He pulled out a lighter and began to light the wick.

Angel swallowed hard. 'Don't be a fool, Glazer,' he yelled. 'If you kill us, you'll be on the run for murder *again*! And when you're caught, you'll *die* in prison!'

Glazer wasn't listening.

The cloth wick caught fire.

Angel heard a woman's voice yell: 'Come on, Eddie.'

Glazer swung his arm back and then lobbed it beyond Spencer among the big pile of straw at the back of the barn.

The bottle exploded, the petrol spread and the vapour ignited creating a loud explosive whoop. The flames took hold of the petrol soaked straw and were instantly three feet high.

Glazer grinned like a devil and disappeared out of sight.

Angel looked across at Gawber who was as alarmed as he was. He saw Spencer suddenly waken up, observe the wall of flames advancing towards him. His eyes flashed as his body thrashed about the post and he cried out for help.

The ferocity of the blaze made a loud humming noise as the fire turned the straw into glowing white and yellow flames. The flames tracked along the barn floor and then roared upwards. Loose bits of straw danced around the parched barn floor around Angel's feet, caught in the under-current of air sucked in by the colossal heat behind him.

Angel struggled to get free of the rope but it was to no avail. He looked at Spencer who was nearest to the flames and tugged harder at the rope. He felt the surge of fresh air pass by him into the far end of the barn drawn in to replace the oxygen already consumed by the fire.

He fought the ropes that tied his hands. It was useless. His wrists grew sore and tired. His face burned and his eyes smarted as the heat built up.

Gawber looked across at him. He began to cough. The fumes were getting to his chest. Angel wanted to call across and say something encouraging and comforting, but he couldn't spit the words out.

The roar of the blaze was so close and loud as to cut out all other sound.

Angel thought of Mary. He might never see her on this earth again. He felt angry and exhausted, but there was nothing else he could do. He began to cough. He felt dizzy and his breathing was becoming difficult. His chest hurt. His throat was sore and dry. He closed his eyes. There was no more pain. He felt nothing. He began to hallucinate. He imagined that his hands had come loose from behind his back and that he was being dragged out of the barn by two men, one each side. His own legs began to work and with their support, he stumbled forward. He opened his eyes and he could see a gravel drive and two men in police riot gear, one each side of him. They were holding onto him by his arms. He was alive. He tried to speak. Instead he croaked. He tried to swallow. His throat was burning. He heard voices.

'His eyes are open, John.'

'Good. Put him down here. He'll get some air.'

Two men lowered him gently on to the gravel drive.

Angel closed his eyes. Next time he opened them, he saw the same two men putting Gawber at his side. He saw him blink and heard him cough. He smiled, and then his eyelids slammed shut like a prison cell door.

CHAPTER ELEVEN

There was a hissing noise. A line of oxygen was blowing gently under his nose. He opened his eyes. He blinked and rubbed his eyes. He noticed an identity tag round his wrist and frowned. He looked up. He was on a bed surrounded by green curtains. He licked his lips. His mouth felt like a bag of feathers. He tried to swallow. It wasn't easy … like swallowing a red hot piece of coke.

A curtain whisked open and a young nurse appeared.

'Ah. You're awake. How are you feeling? Got a headache? Got a pain anywhere?' the nurse said.

'Has my sergeant, Ron Gawber, been brought here?' he croaked.

'He's in the next cubicle. Have you any pain anywhere?'

'Is he all right?'

'Have you any pain anywhere?' she said again, wheeling up a blood pressure machine.

'No,' he croaked irritably. 'Is he all right?'

'Yes. You can have a cup of tea after I've taken your blood pressure.'

'Can I see him?'

'*After* I've taken your blood pressure,' she said wrapping the plastic sleeve round his arm.

Angel took a deep breath and croaked as loudly as he could. 'Are you there, Ron?'

There was silence.

The nurse said, 'I think he's gone back to sleep.'

The plastic sleeve began to inflate.

'Ron,' he bellowed. 'Are you there?'

The nurse pulled a face. 'You'll have to keep still,' she said impatiently.

'Yes, I'm here,' a small husky voice replied. 'I'm all right, sir.'

It was Gawber. Angel's face brightened.

'What about Spencer?' Angel said.

'Keep still,' the nurse snapped.

'Don't know about him,' Gawber said.

Angel turned to the nurse. 'There's a man called Spencer. Is he in here?'

'Don't know anything about him,' she said.

The machine stopped pumping air, clicked and the sleeve began to deflate. She noted the numbers on the dial and began to unwrap the sleeve.

'Still a bit high. You'll have to rest a bit. There's a policeman outside, wants to see you. He can't stay above a minute or so. Now, do you want a cup of tea?'

'Yes, please.'

She wheeled the machine out through the curtain.

Angel whisked back the blanket that was covering him. He was pleased to find that he was fully dressed in all but his shoes. His tie had been loosened and his collar button undone. He leaned over the side of the bed, looking for his shoes when he saw White's head sticking through the curtains.

'Ah, Waldo,' Angel said brightly.

'Are you all right?'

'Yes. Course I am. Did you catch them?'

'No. Could only have been seconds behind though.'

Angel sighed and pulled a face.

White continued: 'We searched the house. It was obvious they'd left in a hurry. There was a half-eaten meal on the table. The front door wasn't even closed. I called the ambulance and the fire brigade.'

'What about Spencer? The other man in the barn.'

'Don't know. He was in a bad way. Been taken to the burns unit. Was he one of the gang?'

Angel shook his head.

'How did the fire start?'

'Eddie Glazer. He intended murdering us.'

'Damn well near managed it. Still, now that you've found their hideout and unseated them, they'll be easier to catch.'

'They'll be more desperate, Waldo.' Angel said grimly.

'Aye, but they'll be floundering round trying to find another safe place to hide. Eddie Glazer is wanted for murder. He knows that every copper in the country has seen his picture and is on the look-out for him. Your super should be chuffed with the news.'

Angel wrinkled his nose. Nothing much pleased Superintendent Harker. 'That gang's got to be caught!' he said. 'They're armed to the teeth, desperate and very, very gung-ho. They could do a lot of damage.'

The nurse appeared with a beaker of tea. She placed it on the locker top, looked up at White and said, 'You'll have to go now. He's got to get some rest.'

Angel caught White's eye, then he looked at the young woman and said, 'I need my shoes, nurse. Where are they?'

'You don't need those yet. Lie back and drink your tea.'

'I want to go to the lavatory,' he said tetchily.

'Stay there. I'll bring you a commode,' she said and rushed off.

Angel's jaw dropped.

However, by the time the nurse had arrived back wheeling an uncomfortable looking tubular metal chair, Angel and Gawber had found their shoes in their respective lockers, and were going down in the hospital lift with DI White.

'Will you take us back to the rhubarb sheds?' Angel said. 'My car is there, and I want to see if the tracking device on Glazer's car is still sending out a signal.'

'Sure. I have to go there, anyway. I need to check on my men. I left them there securing the property.'

'And can I borrow your mobile?'

White handed it to him. He phoned Ahmed and asked him to inform Don Taylor of SOCO that he wanted him to go over the farmhouse where Glazer had been hiding out. He told Ahmed that Taylor was to check in particular for any clothing or effects there that were bloodstained; essentially, he was looking for blood samples that belonged to the late Harry Harrison. Also to see what fingerprints he could collect that would identify Ox and Kenny, if they were on record.

He returned the mobile to White gratefully.

A few minutes later, White dropped Angel and Gawber off at the gate to the rhubarb sheds where he cordially took his leave of them. They gave him hearty thanks and waved him off as he turned round and drove away.

Angel was anxious to return to the scanner to find out the whereabouts of Glazer's Mercedes. He dashed over to his car and unlocked it; Gawber sat beside him, picked up the scanner and switched it on. It showed that the battery of the miniature transmitter was very much alive and sending out a strong signal.

'Looks all right,' Gawber said.

Angel nodded approvingly.

Gawber checked the co-ordinates and then frowned. He said: 'The car hasn't moved, sir. I don't think it has moved since we tracked it here.'

Angel pursed his lips. 'They can't *still* be here?' he said. 'The Merc must be in one of these sheds then?' His face changed as he considered the possibilities. 'That means they're in another car?'

Gawber blinked.

'We've got to find that Merc,' Angel said. 'Come on!'

He dashed out of the car, slammed the door and began to climb over the fence onto the earth trodden track around the sheds. Gawber joined him.

'Doesn't look as if many cars or trucks come in and out of here. We've only got to find recent tyre tracks. That'll not be too difficult. How many sheds are there? Maybe twenty. We've just got to find recent tracks of a car leading out of a pair of doors, that's all.'

True enough. It didn't take them five minutes. The double doors of one of the sheds were locked with a sturdy padlock. The hasps were bolted through thin, old timber. A few kicks and some pulling away of splintering wood permitted them easy access. They dragged open the doors and saw that the shed was empty, but there were tyre tracks in trodden down earth.

'There must be another shed they used as a garage,' Gawber said.

Angel rubbed his chin.

Then he saw something shine on the ground near the door. He bent down and picked it up; it was the tracking device. It must have dropped off the Mercedes. Sometimes this happened if the original fitting to the bodywork had not been made between two clean pieces of metal. This had clearly occurred here.

Angel sighed. All that work, time and endurance counted for nothing. The muscles of his jaw tightened. There would be no further signal from the Mercedes. The Glazer gang were free and could now be committing murder and mayhem totally unrestrained. They had to be found and imprisoned quickly. He raced back to the car, unlocked the door, grabbed the mike of the RT and spoke directly to the operations room at Bromersley station. He gave the duty officer a description of Glazer's Mercedes and index number and told him to circulate all 43 forces with an urgent request for any sighting of it to be made direct back to him on his mobile phone. He added the important warning that Glazer's gang was in possession of the vehicle, that they were armed and extremely dangerous.

'What?' he roared. 'So you have no idea where they are?'

'I am afraid not, sir,' Angel said.

He knew he was going to have to take some stick from Harker.

The superintendent wrinkled his nose and sniffed. 'You know, I much prefer the one about *The Three Bears*,' he growled.

Angel continued unbowed: 'I've had a notice circulated round all 43 forces, sir. Full description and details. Now that Glazer's gang haven't a safe haven to flee to, as they spend their funds, they may have to show their hand.'

'Aye. Probably open an account with the Northern Bank,' he said. 'At two o'clock in the morning,' he added sarcastically. 'What about Spencer? What sort of shape is he in? Where is he now?'

'Pretty bad, sir. But he's in the burns unit at Bromersley General.'

Harker pulled a face that made his big ginger eyebrows bounce up and then down. 'Are you going to be able to make the case of murder against him stick?'

'I don't know, sir. The motive's strong enough.'

'What was he doing in Glazer's gang?'

'He wasn't in the gang, sir. He was their prisoner. They must have wanted something from him.'

'Oh? Information about the bank?'

'More likely about the two million.'

'But Spencer didn't know where Harrison had hidden it.'

'No, sir, but *Glazer* didn't know that.'

Harker rubbed his chin. 'But how did he know about its existence in the first place?'

'Could only have been told about it by Harrison or Spencer.'

'They would have been fools to have told Eddie Glazer.'

'Harrison would have been too smart to have breathed a word about it. But Spencer was comparatively green. Maybe he was scared. Maybe they scared it out of him. As a matter of fact, Glazer told me that Spencer had confessed to him that he had killed Harrison. Said he'd told him he'd stabbed him five times. Five times. He made a point of saying that.'

Harker blinked. 'Have you seen Mac's PM on Harrison? My copy arrived this morning.'

'Not yet, sir.'

'Mac does say that there were *five* separate stabbing wounds to the heart and aorta, delivered in quick succession.'

Angel frowned. 'That would result in a mighty great surge of blood. That suggests that Glazer did it. I can't imagine that if Spencer put a knife into a man intending to murder him, that he could take it out in the midst of blood pumping out and insert it again and again and then twice more. It takes a certain callous, hardened character to do that. And then having succeeded with the murder, be able to recall accurately how many stabs he had made.'

'Hmm. Interesting reasoning, Angel. Reasonable, I suppose. But I fear that wouldn't be enough for the CPS.'

'No sir. If I can get supporting evidence, sir … blood on his clothing … DNA … and so on, they would. Anyway, I have it in hand. SOCO are going through the farmhouse where Glazer's gang were holed up, and which they left in such a hurry.'

Harker nodded. 'Yes. Yes. All right. Give it a go.'

Angel was surprised to get Harker's easy accord. He usually went against everything he said. Angel thought Harker must be in a good mood and, unusually, enjoying a good patch with his wife, Morvydd, an unusual woman. Angel had met her once at a Police Federation Dinner. He hadn't enjoyed the experience. She was almost as objectionable as her husband. He recalled that she had pressed close up to him, smelling of pickled onions, spraying half-chewed Ritz biscuits onto his new dicky, while gushingly insisting that he called her Morvydd. It had taken almost the entire evening to shake her off and get back to the protection of his wife, Mary.

'I've made thorough inquiries along all that end of Wells Street, sir,' Scrivens said brightly.

Angel looked up from his desk, licked his lips and grunted.

'I showed a copy of the photograph in the newspaper shop, the butcher's and the post office nearby, and no one saw anybody that looked like her. They all said that they would have remembered if they had seen anybody like *that*. A woman in the butcher's said the dress looked as if it was from the 1920's. I hung around the steps of the baths, at the critical times of ten minutes to two and eight minutes past three, the times when the taxi driver had collected her and delivered her back, and I showed the photograph to everybody coming through the turnstile, but nobody had seen her. It's hopeless, sir.'

'Right lad. Not to worry. I'm beginning to wonder if she existed at all,' he said, rubbing his chin. 'Or was she a cardboard cut-out like the Cottingley fairies,' he added quietly.

'The Cottingley fairies, sir?' Scrivens said.

'Oh?' Angel looked up. He was surprised that Scrivens had heard him. 'The Cottingley fairies never existed, lad. They were paper cut-outs of fairies that were photographed by two mischievous young ladies from Cottingley – it's not far away, near Bradford. But they let the world believe they were the real thing.'

'Fairies, sir?' He laughed. 'Who would believe that?'

Angel's face was as straight as a copper's truncheon. 'The photographs fooled several distinguished people at the time.' He sniffed, then sighed and said: 'Just like – I do believe – Lady Blessington, whoever she is, is fooling us right now!'

Scrivens frowned.

'And it's getting right up my nose,' Angel added with his lips tightening. 'And wasting a lot of police time, when I am up to my neck in it.'

Scrivens scratched his head.

'Yes, sir. Do you want me to do anything else?'

'Yes, lad. I want you to go to the burns unit at the hospital, and beg, borrow or steal Simon Spencer's clothes. Don't take "no" from the hospital staff. If you have to, point out that this is a murder inquiry. I want everything he was wearing when he was admitted yesterday, including his shoes. Put them carefully in an evidence bag, seal it and take it round to Don Taylor at the SOCO office. Tell him I want him to see if there is any DNA of Harry Harrison anywhere on them. I am particularly looking for traces of his blood. If there is anything, then we've potentially got Spencer for murder. All right?'

Scriven's nodded enthusiastically.

'Right, sir.'

He went out.

Angel looked at the mountain of post, reports and general bumf piled up in front of him and blew out a long sigh. He began fingering through it. He wasn't looking for anything specific. He was hoping that he could find some inconsequential big lump that he could drop into the waste-paper basket to make the pile instantly smaller. It was not to be. He came across an envelope from the General Hospital, Bromersley. He quickly slit it open. It was Mac's post-mortem on Harry Harrison aka Harry Henderson. He raced through it and noted that the small clumps of hair found on Harrison's coat were his own and thought to have been pulled out of his scalp in the course of a fight; there were many bruises to his head and chest areas as the result of a number of blows thought to have been delivered by bare knuckles. All the blood samples taken at the scene also belonged to the victim.

Angel reread the pertinent facts and grunted unhappily. He could see nothing in the report that would immediately indicate the identity of Harrison's murderer. He nodded as he considered that the victim's assailant, if it was one person, would almost certainly have very bruised knuckles. He sighed and began pushing the report back into the envelope when there was a knock at the door.

It was Ahmed. He came in waving an evidence envelope. 'DS Taylor dropped these in, sir. Mrs Prophet's address book and a Christmas card list. He said you were expecting them.'

Angel took them eagerly. 'Right, lad. Thank you.'

Ahmed went out.

Angel opened the envelope and tipped the two items out onto the desk. He looked carefully down the Christmas card list, which wasn't dated, then looked through the address book. It was a small but thick, leather-backed book with many crossings out, additions and alterations. He looked firstly at the B's for Blessington to no avail, then at the C's, just in case she had been entered under C for Cora, but there was no entry there either. He leaned back from the desk and shook his head.

There was a knock at the door. It was DS Gawber.

Angel looked up. He was pleased to see him. 'Feeling OK.'

'Bit of a sore throat, sir. All that smoke.'

'Yeah. Yeah. Sit down.'

'Have I missed anything, sir?'

'I was just looking in Alicia Prophet's address book for an entry for Lady Blessington. Of course, there isn't one,' he said glumly. He pointed at the chair and rubbed his chin.

Gawber sat down. He nodded his understanding at Angel's disappointment.

Angel's eyes narrowed. 'This case is really infuriating me, Ron,' he said, grinding his teeth. 'We are just not getting anywhere. Let's kick it about a bit.'

Gawber nodded. That's what Angel always did when he'd reached an impasse.

'A so-called friend of the family, Lady Blessington,' Angel said, 'with a title, although we now know that's false, and also there's no entry of her in Mrs Prophet's address book or on their Christmas card list, called every month. She collected … or took money from Mrs Prophet, a blind woman … a thousand pounds every month for the last six months.'

'That sounds like rent or blackmail, sir,' Gawber said.

Angel nodded to him, then continued. 'But on Monday last, she arrived with a handgun and murdered her.'

'Killed the goose that laid the golden egg?'

'Exactly, but why?'

'Does Lady B stand to inherit anything, sir?'

'No Ron, she doesn't. It all goes to the husband. That's another one of the things that doesn't make sense. Lady B hasn't a motive. If she does, I don't know what it is. If she was milking Alicia Prophet to the tune of a thousand quid a month, why kill her? The husband says he knew Lady B only slightly. However we know that he took a photograph of her, having tea with his wife on their patio. I have the very photograph.'

He plunged into his pocket and took out the photograph still covered in polythene and placed it on the desk.

'Anyway, Lady B arrived on Monday afternoon by taxi, having been picked up from the baths on Wells Street. She was seen walking up the garden path and entering the house. About an hour later, she was seen running from the house to the taxi. The taxi driver says he took her back to Well Street Baths where she then disappeared into outer space and has never been seen since.'

'But she shot Alicia Prophet, sir?' Gawber said decisively.

'Without a doubt. There's nobody else. The husband would be the expected murderer. But he has an excellent alibi. He was working in his office with his secretary.'

'Very beautiful secretary, you said, sir,' he said pointedly.

'Yes, all right. Very beautiful secretary,' Angel said irritably. 'Now there are several witnesses to Lady B dashing out of the house only a minute or so before Mrs Prophet's dead body was found by Mrs Duplessis, a neighbour, on the settee, with orange peel scattered hither and thither.'

'Same MO as Reynard.'

'No prints or DNA left by the murderer. There is £6.56 in cash found on the draining board. Fresh oranges, bought locally, are found in the dustbin … two bags of shopping in the pantry doorway. And Lady B looks like an older version of the model in a painting found on the wall of Margaret Gaston's bedroom.'

'Who is she, sir? The girl in the painting?'

'An unknown model from the 1930s.'

'It couldn't have been Lady B when she was younger?'

'No. She would have had to have been born in 1910.'

'Of course. Could it have been her mother?'

Angel blinked. 'Witnesses put Lady B between forty and sixty. Yes. If you stretch things a bit, it's possible. I suppose it could be her mother, but that doesn't give us a motive for her murdering Alicia Prophet? Nor an indication as to where she has disappeared to.'

Gawber shook his head. 'No sir. But there must some reason why this picture turns up at this time. It's telepathy. It's a telepathic picture of the murderer. Do you think somebody or something out there is … trying to tell us something?'

Angel pulled a face and ran his hand quickly through his hair. 'Don't let's get carried away, Ron. You can't solve murders with a ouija board, tarot cards and magic smoke writing!'

'But there must be an explanation,' Gawber said forcefully.

'Yes,' Angel said animatedly. 'I am sure there is. I don't know what it is yet, but there *will* be a reason, and I bet it's a damn good reason too.'

'Or it could be coincidence.'

'*Coincidence*?' he yelled. '*Coincidence*! How many times have I told you, Ron. When you look for evidence in a murder case, there's no such thing as coincidence!'

Gawber didn't reply. He didn't want to annoy Angel further, so he decided to stay silent.

There was an awkward silence.

Angel was a little embarrassed by having allowed himself to be unnecessarily irritated and worked up over what he considered to be Gawber's unorthodox attitude to coincidences. He considered briefly whether to apologize or not, decided against it, then returned to the original problem in hand. He rubbed his chin thoughtfully.

Eventually, he broke the silence and said: 'What's so fascinating about blue, Ron?'

'Blue, sir? The colour blue?'

'Yes. Lady Blessington is always seen in the same blue dress.'

'Maybe she's only got one best dress? She's hard up. No shame in being poor, sir.'

'No. None at all. Still I think if she's visiting Bromersley, and been around here for six months, you'd think she'd want to show the world an alternative dress … if only to follow the seasons round?'

'I expect so, sir. Even I have two suits. Sunday best, and second best.'

'In the winter, if she only had one dress, she could wear something – a coat or a cloak – over it, I suppose, couldn't she?'

'That dress would show under her coat.'

'Aye. Why does she wear such a long dress, Ron? After all, it's the middle of summer. The temperature has … sometimes … been in the eighties.'

'Maybe she's got lousy legs, sir.'

'You mean muscular?'

'Don't know what I mean. I'm just thinking aloud, sir.'

'Do you think she was sporty?'

'Yes, sir. She caught the taxi to and from the swimming baths on Wells Road. Maybe she was a swimmer?'

'I don't know. She wasn't seen in the pool on the CCTV, you know. But some sporty women have powerful limbs that are not necessarily attractive.'

'That dress covered her arms as well.'

'Yes, well maybe she's also got great muscular arms?'

'Maybe. Maybe.'

The door suddenly opened. It was Ahmed. He didn't knock. There was something different about him. His eyes were shining.

'Have you heard the news, sir?'

'What?' Angel looked up and snapped at him.

'Reynard's been arrested and charged, sir. It's on TV. It was a news flash. I was in the canteen.'

Angel and Gawber leapt to their feet and rushed out of the office and up the corridor to the double doors and through to the station canteen. There was a crowd of ten policemen and women looking up at the TV fastened high up to the wall. They rushed up and stood behind them.

On the screen, they could see a man in a plain dark suit standing in front of a stone building speaking directly to camera. Underneath him was a caption that read: 'Detective Inspector Blenkinsop.' He was saying:

'... known as Reynard, aged 35 years of Cutforth Road, London SW, was at 0935 hours this morning arrested after an exchange of gunfire outside the Chitterton branch of the Exchange Building Society. The arrest came after a week-long surveillance operation by the Serious Organised Crime Agency of the police, and demonstrates how successful the police can be, when the different forces under the direction of SOCA can work together to fight crime.'

CHAPTER TWELVE

Angel slowly put the phone back in its cradle. He smiled, turned to Gawber and said, 'That was DI Blenkinsop of Chitterton CID. He confirms that they have had Reynard under observation for the past six days and that there is no possible chance that he could have been anywhere near Creeford Road on Monday afternoon last.'

Gawber nodded and smiled. 'So that clears that up. The orange peel found around Alicia Prophet's body, was definitely not left there by Reynard.'

'That's right,' Angel said rubbing his hands gleefully.

Gawber frowned. 'So we have to find out why Lady B left it. Are we to suppose that, like Reynard, she had to have a swift intake of vitamin C every time she murdered somebody?'

Angel stopped rubbing his hands, pursed his lips and said, 'I have an idea about that, Ron, but at the moment, I can't make it all fit.'

'But Lady B *did* shoot Alicia Prophet, sir, didn't she? She *was* the last person to see Mrs Prophet alive?'

'I believe so.' He reached up to his ear and massaged the lobe of it slowly between finger and thumb. He sighed and added: 'But I am not happy about how we arrive at that conclusion.'

'Witnesses, sir. Three witnesses.'

'Yes, Ron. But the clues are all wrong. I mean … why do you think we are provided with a woman in a blue dress who makes herself very well known to the husband, a neighbour and a taxi driver, so that, after she has murdered Mrs Prophet, those very witnesses are in a position to describe her to us in such absolute detail?'

'I don't understand, sir,' Gawber said.

'Well, we have a full description of her, yet after the taxi driver drops her back at Wells Road Baths, we are unable to trace her? And you know something else, Ron. I bet you that we'll never see Lady Cora Blessington again. Charles Prophet smelled a rat, and warned his wife against her. She should have heeded his warnings. A murderer worth his salt would not want to be known by his name, much less be recognized by the victim's spouse, two neighbours *and* a taxi-driver.'

Gawber looked into Angel's eyes. He admired his clear, logical thinking. Here was the inspector at his very best.

'No, it's all wrong, Ron,' Angel continued. 'Instinct screams out at me. This is a very unusual case. We are dealing with a very clever and dangerous individual, who is very close to us. I feel it in my bones. We are being had, Ron. Lady B or whoever she is, is making monkeys out of us, and I don't like it!'

Gawber rubbed his chin. 'Well, where is she now, sir? She can't have disappeared into thin air?'

'No, she hasn't. She's really very close. She has discarded the blue dress, hat and trainers, and is now dressed in normal, everyday clothes, working in an office, factory or shop; driving a car, a truck or pushing a pram; looking after a husband, a family or whatever life she has made for herself.'

'All right, sir, but what's her motive?'

'Money. She began to milk Alicia Prophet for all the money she could. And that's quite a lot, but when the poor woman realized that that was what she was about, she turned off the tap and Lady B snapped. In the absence of any other information, that's the motive.'

Gawber frowned and rubbed his chin. 'Well, where do we go from here.'

'Back to the beginning, where else? We need to go back and interview all the witnesses. Check through all the evidence, look at the murder in an entirely different light. This is the unusual case of the murderer who *wanted* to be recognized.'

Gawber shook his head. 'But we don't know who she is. It's all very complicated. Maybe we'll never find the murderer.'

'Oh, we'll find the murderer all right.'

'If she gets away with it, it will go down as the perfect crime.'

Angel raised his head. His bottom lip jutted forward defiantly. 'There is no such thing as the perfect crime!'

Angel reached the top step, held onto the banister rail and breathed heavily. Those three flights of stairs had played havoc with the calves of his legs. He stood there to catch his breath, remembering with satisfaction that even though he was breathing a bit heavily, he had given up smoking finally three years earlier. He looked across the landing at the door with the number 19 stuck on it: that was Margaret Gaston's flat. He listened out for banging drums and raucous electronic racket, but all was quiet. He was approaching the door, when it opened unexpectedly. A man wearing a crumpled grey suit, light-coloured, open-necked shirt, grey hair and a broad smile came out. He closed the door quietly then turned round. When he saw Angel, he gasped, his eyes lit up and the smile vanished; he put a hand across his mouth and nose and dashed past him down the stairs. Angel didn't recognize him but he knew when a man looked guilty. And that man looked very guilty. His eyes followed the little man until he disappeared round the bend in the staircase. He turned back and noticed a wicked smell of brandy, then, thoughtfully, he crossed the landing and knocked on the door; it was promptly opened by Margaret Gaston. She was smiling.

'Forgotten something, Luke?' she said quickly. 'Oh.'

'Hello.'

When she saw it was Angel, the smile left her. Her eyes flashed and her face flushed up scarlet. She quickly closed the door to an opening of ten inches or so.

Through the gap, Angel could see that the top half of her was cosily wrapped in a short, quilted housecoat, but her long legs were uncovered down to her feet, which were snugly enclosed in the rabbit skin slippers.

'Oh, I … I thought it was … somebody else,' she stammered, closing the door another inch or two.

Angel put his hand on the door to keep it open.

She maintained the pressure on her side to narrow the gap.

'I need to ask you a few more questions, Margaret. It won't take long.'

'I'm afraid it's not convenient just now.'

'Why? Have you something in there you don't want me to see?'

'No. No,' she said, trying to be nonchalant. 'I was just going to … take a bath, that's all.'

Angel applied more pressure on the door.

'The bath can wait. It'll only take five minutes.'

Her face hardened. 'Have you got a warrant?' she said sternly.

The question quite surprised him. His eyebrows shot up. 'I don't need a warrant just to talk to you, Margaret,' he said applying more pressure on the door. 'What are you afraid of?'

'Nothing,' she said quickly. 'Nothing.' She suddenly pulled the door open wide. She knew she couldn't win. 'I'm not properly dressed for visitors,' she said. 'That's all.'

Angel smiled wryly. She wasn't properly dressed last time he interviewed her. She didn't object to his presence then, so what was different?

He glanced round the room to see what it was that she may not have wanted him to see. He saw a part bottle of Napoleon brandy and a glass on the sideboard. Underneath the bottle placed in the shape of a fan were three, ten pound notes.

She dashed over to the sideboard. He saw her pick up the notes, fold them and deftly stuff them into her bra. Then she quickly picked up the bottle and glass, turned round to face him, switched on a smile, rocked the bottle invitingly and said: 'Drinkie?'

He shook his head.

'Oh no. Of course. You're on duty,' she said tartly. 'Well, sit down, Michael,' she said. 'Won't be a second.'

She shuffled off in the slippers into the kitchen, deposited the bottle and glass and came out with a packet of Silk Cut and a disposable lighter. She glanced down at the cot as she passed it to the sofa to check that baby Carl was asleep, she smiled briefly, then flopped athletically onto the sofa stretching out her long legs.

'I thought you might have brought my picture back,' she said as she tore off the cellophane from around the packet.

'Er, no. I hope you don't mind. I'd like to keep it until the case is solved, if that's all right. Your landlady doesn't mind.'

'Right,' she said crisply.

Angel took out an envelope from his inside pocket and pretended to read it. He tried to marshal his thoughts.

She tapped out a cigarette and lit it. She blew out a big cloud of tobacco smoke. 'Well, what is it you want to ask me?' she said.

'Who was that man?' he said without looking up.

She thought a moment then said, 'Nobody.' Then she slapped down the lighter boldly and blew out another big cloud.

He continued to look down at the envelope. 'How long have you known him?'

'Who?'

'Mr Nobody.'

'Oh, him?' There was another pause. 'He came to check the gas oven and the boiler. Make sure it doesn't give off CO^2, and gas us while we were asleep.'

'He reeked of brandy,' he sniffed. 'So do you. Do you entertain all your visitors with brandy?'

'We just got carried away,' she said with a grin.

'Brandy is expensive.'

'So what? I didn't buy it, Michael. He brought it.'

Angel shook his head. 'He brought a bottle of brandy to check on your gas boiler?'

She took a drag on the cigarette and breathed out loudly. 'All right, Michael. All right. So he didn't call to check the bloody boiler, but he has absolutely nothing to do with the murder of Alicia Prophet. He's just a sweet little man who visits me almost every Friday in his lunch hour. Now, I don't want you investigating him and upsetting his job or his wife. If any of this leaks out you could wreck his marriage!'

'How long has this been going on?'

'About a year.'

He sighed and shook his head. 'What's his surname?'

'I can't tell you *that*!' she exploded.

'Well, I daresay we will be able to find him easily enough. There won't be many Lukes working at the gas board.'

'I don't want your men climbing all over the bloody gas board offices, Michael. You'll give him away as easy as wink. He's a quiet, nervous little man. He relies on me to be discreet. It's not fair.'

Angel sighed. 'Look here, Margaret, life isn't fair. You have to do the best you can. But if you don't do anything wrong, you can tell the truth, the complete truth, can't you?'

'Yes. Yes,' she said irritably. She didn't like being lectured. 'Now what were those questions you wanted to ask me?'

'What's his name?'

She shook her head.

Angel said: 'If his only crime is being unfaithful to his wife, I tell you, Margaret, I am not a bit interested … probably won't even need to check him out.'

She sighed: 'Luke Molloy.'

'Thank you.'

The name didn't ring any bells with him. He scribbled it quickly on the envelope and pushed it into his pocket.

'Now what were those questions you wanted to ask me?' she said impatiently.

'Yes. The afternoon Mrs Prophet was murdered, where were you?'

'That was Monday, wasn't it? I was here. I told you. That's the day I have for doing *my* shopping and that. I don't go to the Prophets' on Mondays.'

'But specifically, Margaret, did you go to the Prophets' house *last* Monday?'

'No.'

'Do you do Mrs Prophet's shopping?'

'Some of it, yes.'

'And did she ask you to do some shopping for her on Monday? I know you did some shopping because you bought some oranges from the man on the market.'

'I told you, I didn't see her on Monday.'

'Well, she could have phoned you or left a message or asked you earlier.'

'Well, she could have, but she didn't.'

'You see, Margaret, there was some shopping left in the doorway of Prophet's pantry.'

She shrugged.

'And some money, £6.56,' Angel said. 'Could have been change from the shopping, left on the draining board in the kitchen?'

'Could have been done by Mrs Duplessis, next door. She shopped for her sometimes. In fact, she was always dropping in. Pain in the backside, she was.'

Angel nodded. That might be true.

'But you had shopped for Mrs Prophet in the past, hadn't you?'

'Yes. Regular. At least once a week. Usually a Wednesday.'

'Ah,' he said enthusiastically, 'now where would you have left the shopping and the change in the event of Mrs Prophet being out when you returned?'

'Alicia was never out. She never went out. It would have driven me bats. She didn't want to go out. What would have been the point? She couldn't see anything.'

'Well, humour me,' he said.

She shrugged. 'If Alicia had been out, the house would have been locked up. I would have had to have brought her shopping here. And, before you ask, I wouldn't have been able to get into Alicia's, *because I haven't got a key*!'

Angel wrinkled his nose and rubbed his chin.

Her raised voice in answering the question might have disturbed Carl. There was a slight noise from the cot. It sounded as if he was waking up and wasn't too pleased about it. She leaped up from the sofa, flashing the long legs and stabbing her feet into the rabbit slippers.

'He's waking up.'

Angel looked across at mother leaning over the cot and baby Carl, whose bottom lip was turned down and his face creased. There was a second's delay then a loud cry began the most woeful time of howling.

Margaret picked him up. 'Aaaah. There's my beautiful little boy,' she said. 'There, now. There. There.'

She jiggled him in her arms but the crying continued.

'He wants some juice, Michael. He's teething.'

Angel put out his arms. 'Give him to me. He'll be all right with me, won't you Carl? I'll hold him. Go and get some him some juice, Margaret.'

Carl's eyes focused on Angel. He looked willing to go to him.

'Come on, Carl,' Angel said warmly. 'Come on, big boy.'

He held out his arms and Margaret handed him across. 'He'll mucky up your suit,' she warned.

'No matter. It'll clean. *There* we are,' Angel said, nestling him on his knee.

Magically, the crying stopped.

Margaret grinned at the big man holding the baby so close to him and began to tickle his nose with a finger.

'Won't be a minute,' she said.

'No rush,' Angel said. 'We're all right, aren't we, Carl? We can get along a treat, can't we? Yes we can. Yes we can. Cutgee, cutgee, cutgee coo. Cutgee, cutgee, cutgee coo....'

Margaret smiled and disappeared into the kitchen.

The toddler's mouth was very moist.

Angel looked round for a tissue. There were none to hand, so took a new handkerchief out of his breast pocket, shook it open and wiped Carl's lips dry. However, there was more dribble, a lot more. Carl dribbled mightily into it. Angel folded it, wiped the little boy's lips dry again, folded it over again and pushed it back into his breast pocket.

Margaret came back in with a plastic feeding cup.

Carl looked up at her with the cup and lifted up his arms. That was what he needed. She gave him the cup, he took it eagerly, then she lifted him off Angel's knee.

Angel was reluctant to have Carl taken from him. He smiled as he looked down at the little lad on his mother's knee, noisily sucking at the juice.

Angel walked up the path, pressed the illuminated bell push on the door surround, stood back and waited.

The door was opened after a short delay, by the lady of the house, who peered at him cautiously. 'Yes?' she said adjusting her spectacles.

'Good afternoon, Mrs Duplessis,' Angel said. 'Could I have a word?'

'Oh, it's Inspector Angel,' she said, looking relieved. 'Why, of course. Of course. Please come in,' she replied.

She conducted him to her sitting-room.

'Just a couple of things I need to clear up.'

'Yes. Yes. Anything I can do to help.'

'I understand that from time to time, you did some shopping for Mrs Prophet?'

'Yes. Well, I would have done anything to help her. Poor woman.'

'Well, last Monday, the day of the murder ... did you do any shopping for her or Mr Prophet?'

'No,' she said. 'I remember in the morning asking if she needed anything, but she said that Margaret was bringing in some bits and would drop them in on her way back from the shops.'

Angel frowned. 'You see, there was unpacked shopping in two bags on the floor in the pantry and some money, presumably change, on the draining board.'

'That would have been Margaret. Though I'm surprised she didn't put the shopping away. Mrs Prophet could have tripped over it. She knew not to leave stuff lying around on the floor.'

Angel's face dropped. He didn't like the answer. 'And the money on the draining board?'

'That was the arranged place to leave money or keys or anything like that.'

'But Margaret didn't work for the Prophets on Mondays.'

'That's right, but Mrs Prophet knew that Margaret did her own shopping on Mondays and sometimes asked her to drop a few things in. After all, she has to pass the back gate from town up to Mansion Hill. It wasn't out of her way.'

'She would use the back door then? Hmm. So if she had come in to the Prophets' house, you wouldn't have seen her?'

'No, I didn't see her. I wouldn't from my house. She would simply go through the gate, up the path, knock on the door, open it, call out and go in. That was the usual routine. It was the most considerate way, really, with Alicia being blind.'

'Hmm.'

'I might add that Lady Blessington simply walked straight in when she came visiting. She never, *ever* knocked.'

Angel blinked. 'Really? Hmmm. The thing is, Mrs Duplessis, about Margaret Gaston, she *says* she didn't call at the house on Monday, the day of the murder. She's quite adamant about it.'

Mrs Duplessis sighed, shook her head and said, 'Frankly, Inspector, she must be ... mistaken.'

'You mean she lying?'

'I didn't want to be so … confrontational, Inspector, but I can't think of any other … explanation.'

Angel pursed his lips.

CHAPTER THIRTEEN

The shapely Karen Kennedy fluttered her eyelashes, held open the inner office door and said, 'Mr Prophet will see you now, Inspector.'

'Thank you,' Angel said, appreciating the whiff of perfume as he brushed past her.

Charles Prophet was standing, leaning over the desk, his hand already outstretched, ready to welcome him.

'So very pleased to see you, Inspector. Please sit down and make yourself comfortable.'

'Thank you,' Angel said. He noticed the pasty, unhappy face and the noted that he was wearing a black tie.

'Please tell me what progress you are making finding this ... woman,' Prophet said.

'Frankly, Mr Prophet, it isn't easy. But have no fear, we will catch her in due course.'

'You have something of a reputation, Inspector. The word round town is – like the Mounties – you *always* get your man?'

Angel looked at him, but said nothing. What was there to say?

'Or, in this case,' Prophet added, 'your woman.'

'I hope not to fail this time, Mr Prophet,' he said evenly. 'That's why I am here. There are one or two points on which I would like clarification.'

Prophet nodded. 'Of course. Fire away.'

'There's the matter of the description of Lady Blessington. You are probably the person who knew her the best … saw her the most, after your dear wife. Other witnesses say she that she had a squawky voice, unusually high-pitched.'

'I never detected anything unusual in the way she spoke, Inspector. I thought that she spoke perfectly normally: educated, pleasant enough, with no particular accent.'

Angel nodded.

'How old do you think she was?'

'Must have been over sixty, I would have thought.'

Angel rubbed his chin. 'Everybody else thought she was younger: between forty and sixty.'

'Maybe she was. I am, perhaps, not good at assessing ladies' ages. She was always pretending to be something she wasn't. She was clearly unstable to have committed such a heinous crime.' He stopped, swallowed and then added, 'It's hard for me to speak … dispassionately.'

'Of course. Of course. Forgive my asking these sorts of questions.'

'That's all right. You have your job to do and I do want to help.'

'You believe that she murdered your wife because she couldn't extract any more money from her?'

'Convinced of it. What other explanation could there be?'

'I don't know. And have you absolutely no idea where she lived … or where she came from?'

'I believe she said that she had a small cottage in Norfolk.'

Angel looked up interestedly. That was new.

'What part of Norfolk? Did she mention the town?'

'Of course not,' he said wryly.

'Did she come here by train?'

Prophet said: 'I really wasn't interested enough to bother to find out these details, Inspector. I simply wanted her to leave us alone. As I have said, I never liked the woman and tried to put Alicia off her, but poor dear, she was always willing to help anyone who came to her with a sob story. This woman was clearly … deranged.'

'Would it surprise you to learn that she wasn't titled?'

'Nothing about Cora would surprise me.'

'We just can't get a lead on her? Did she ever express any interest in a particular place, apart from Norfolk, where she might have bolted to. She's disappeared off the face of the earth. Any information would be most welcome.'

Prophet wrinkled his nose. 'Alicia once said that she had spoken fondly about the sunshine in Florida, I recall. But that was probably only a passing fancy.'

Angel sighed. Florida was a big state. He hoped that it would not come to contacting the Federal Police over there.

'Well, if you think of anything…?'

'Of course.'

Angel consulted his notes.

'Now, about Margaret Gaston. She said she didn't go to your house that … Monday.'

'She doesn't work for us on Mondays.'

'Did you take any shopping into your wife anytime on that day? There was some shopping found in the pantry and some money, £6.56, found on the draining board in the kitchen.'

Prophet frowned. 'No. It was not I,' he said. 'I had not yet returned to the house after I left for the office on the morning of that dreadful day; still haven't. I'm staying at The Feathers Hotel.'

Angel nodded and said, 'There must be some explanation. Your wife *was* completely blind, wasn't she? She wasn't capable of doing any shopping, was she?'

'Of course not. Mrs Duplessis, next door, may have brought in that shopping, but it sounds more likely to have been Margaret Gaston. My wife may have asked her to shop for some things and to pop them in on her way back from town. And it *was* quite usual for her to put the change and leave any messages on the draining board in the kitchen.'

'Did she have a key?'

'No, but she wouldn't need a key. The door would have been unlocked. Both doors, front and back, were unlocked. It was easier for Alicia, you see.'

'And oranges. Did your wife like oranges?'

'Why, yes, of course,' Prophet said, looking at him with eyebrows raised.

'There were some freshly bought oranges in the outside rubbish bin, and orange peel strewn about the settee. Do you know anything about that?'

'No. Sounds very odd.'

Angel's lips stretched back tight across his teeth as he nodded.

'Lady B was, by all accounts, tall, sir,' Gawber said. 'All the witnesses are quite agreed on that. And *that* picture of her *was* above that girl's bed. Now Margaret Gaston is quite tall. Put that blue dress on her, a wig, the hat and the trainers and, I think we'd have a Lady Blessington look alike. It must have been her. It would explain the shopping in the pantry, the money on the draining board, the orange peel over the body and the oranges in the dustbin?'

'I am satisfied that the orange peel over the body was to try to put the blame for the murder on Reynard, but we now know it couldn't have been him.'

'I realize that, sir.'

'But the lass is ... too beautiful to be Lady B,' he replied thoughtfully. 'And seems to be a lot younger.'

'She could have worn a mask.'

Angel looked up at him. He accepted that that was a possibility.

'She'd probably manage the strained voice all right, Ron,' he said. 'I'll give you that. She'd just have to talk an octave or so higher.'

'And she's very hard up, sir. Desperate for money. You said she was on the game.'

'Aye. Got that little lad, Carl, to bring up, hasn't she? Another one-parent family. Hmmm.'

'It might help if we knew who the father was.'

'It might. It might very well, Ron,' he said heavily and then he stood up. 'I'll think about it over the weekend. Right now, I'm going to the hospital. See Spencer. Then I'm going straight home. I've had enough of this week. See you on Monday.'

The woman at the hospital reception desk directed him to Room 12, Ward 23 on the second floor. He found it, tapped on the door and waited a couple of seconds. There was no reply so he pressed down the handle and walked in.

It was a single room with minimum furniture: bed, locker, chair, sink and a pedestal fan. There was a patient on the bed, not covered by blankets or sheets, but encased in bandages except for the eyes, nose, mouth and hands. Angel assumed it was a man.

The patient was resting on his side on a big pile of pillows on an unusually large bed; he had his knees bent so that he was almost in a foetal position. The fan was blowing a cool breeze over him. As Angel closed the door, he turned his head slightly to look round at his visitor.

'Mr Spencer?' Angel said. 'Simon Spencer?'

'Yes,' the man said, groaning. 'Can you tell me how much longer I am going to be bandaged up like this?'

Angel found the chair.

'I'm not a doctor, Mr Spencer. I'm Detective Inspector Angel.'

'Ooooh,' he moaned.

'You're lucky to be alive.'

'So they tell me,' he said sourly. 'Don't I recognize you? Weren't you and another chap fastened up in Glazer's barn, when that lunatic threw that bomb in it?'

Angel nodded.

'And you're in the police?' His voice indicated that the fact was stretching his belief. 'What do you want with me?'

'I think you know what I want,' he said evenly.

'No,' Spencer said. 'I have no idea. You'll have to spell it out.'

'I am investigating the murder of Harry Harrison also known as Harry Henderson.'

'Well, he *was* a little worm, but good gracious, I didn't have anything to do with *that*.'

'That's what *you* say. We know that you worked a nice little fraudulent gig with him, and for that, you will be charged in due course. What I am interested in today is how Harrison came to be stabbed to death and dumped in a skip on the car park of The Three Horseshoes.'

'Well, Inspector, I don't know anything about *that*.'

Angel looked straight into his eyes.

'Where were you on the night of Monday, July 16th?'

'I can't remember that now. I'm pretty certain that I was at home.'

Angel sniffed. 'And what's the address? If it's 212 Huddersfield Road, don't bother wasting my time.'

Spencer sniggered, then he said, 'I can't remember.'

The muscles of Angel's jaw tightened. 'Well, you'd better start remembering something. You're already going down for fraud. If you don't remember something, you could be looking through steel bars for the rest of your life.'

Angel seemed to have struck a nerve. Spencer's breathing became uneven and his hands began to shake.

'I can't exactly remember everything,' he stammered. 'It's true. I was looking for him. I had to find him to get my share of the money, but he had gone to ground. I had heard he had been seen in that pub, The Three Horseshoes, but when I got there, there was no sign of him.'

'Go on,' Angel said.

'Well, I was making enquiries about him from the landlord. He said he didn't know anything, but a mouthy man, who I later learned was Eddie Glazer, overheard us. He said that he was a friend of Harrison and bought me a drink. I thought he might lead me to him. We were getting on rather well. Then he said he had something special about Harry to show me in his car. I fell for it. We went outside, and I was set on by him and three other thugs, who knocked me out cold. I must have been unconscious for twelve hours. When I woke up, I was in a big house. They locked me in a room. They kept beating me up and throwing cold water over me … and asking me where the money was. I didn't know, did I? If I had known I would have taken my share and disappeared. But they kept on at me. Glazer got big Ox to persuade me – as he called it – but I didn't know anything. They even sent Glazer's wife in to try and coax it out of me. They simply wouldn't believe me. The trouble was that Harrison owed Glazer ten thousand pounds. Something to do with his escape from prison, and the fact that he hadn't paid stuck in Glazer's gullet. Anyway, they held me for three nights, I believe. I lost track of time. I was taken to the barn. The rest you know.'

Angel rubbed his chin. It had the ring of truth about it. He was more than half inclined to believe him. He was still waiting for the results of SOCO's tests on Spencer's and Glazer gang's clothes and effects. He was hopeful of some conclusive evidence that would enable him to make an arrest. It should also indicate whether Spencer was a liar or not. He remembered that SOCO had also reported that Harrison had been severely assaulted with clenched fists before he was stabbed; such an assault would leave abrasions, bruising or scuffs on the assailant's hands and knuckles.

'Hold your hands out,' Angel said.

'What?'

Angel reached out and took hold of one hand. He grabbed it tightly by the wrist.

'Here. What's happening? What are you doing?'

Spencer tried to pull away, but Angel held it with a grip of iron. He looked at the back of his hand and at the knuckles, then turned it over. It felt like a rubber glove stuffed with bread and butter pudding. He took the other hand. It was the same. He sniffed and let both hands drop. They were the hands of a man who had never done a hard day's work in his life, much less been involved in a punch up. But Angel was still not quite satisfied.

'You've no idea who gave Harry Harrison a damned good hiding and finished him off by sticking a knife into him several times, then dumped him in that skip, leaving him to bleed to death, have you?'

'Well, it wasn't me. More than likely it would have been Eddie Glazer. He probably caught up with Harrison in the pub or somewhere and the little squirt refused to tell him where he'd hidden the money. Glazer's a nasty piece of work.'

'Hmmm,' Angel muttered. That was true. 'I'll be frank with you, Spencer,' Angel began. 'Glazer and his gang have disappeared. All we have to go on at the moment is the description and licence plate number of their car. Any assistance you can give me in finding where they might have disappeared to would be greatly appreciated.'

Spencer sighed then said: 'I don't know anything about that, Inspector. Honestly, I haven't a clue. I wish I had. They're no friends of mine.'

Angel was tired and fed up. It was the weekend. Thank God for that. Two murder cases in one week was hard work. He went home. He put the car away, locked the garage, came in through the back door, smiled weakly at Mary, took a bottle of German beer out of the fridge and a glass off the draining-board and shuffled off into the sitting-room. He loosened his tie, pressed a button on the television remote control and slumped into the chair. As the set warmed up it showed a young woman in front of a map rattling off details at high speed about the temperature and global warming. He sipped the beer. It had been five days since he had first been sent to Creesforth Road and had been presented with the murder of Alicia Prophet. He wasn't really any the wiser about the mysterious Lady B. An amateur murderer if ever there was one, he thought. Virtually advertised the fact that she was at the scene of the crime at the time of the murder. Committed the murder in broad daylight, ate an orange and sprayed the peel over the body, then trotted down the front path like a lady of leisure, conveniently dropping her handbag in front of a neighbour, Mrs Duplessis. Made sure the taxi driver would remember her, publicized her destination, Wells Street Baths, then disappeared in a puff of smoke. Ridiculous.

The other case, the murder of Harry Harrison … now *that* was relatively simple. It was committed by one crook or the other. One suspect was in hospital, and with his injuries, he wasn't going anywhere in a hurry. The other was … well … somewhere else.

Mary came in with his tea on a tray. It was finnan haddock. They always had fish on a Friday. He enjoyed that then reached out for the *Radio Times* to see what might be on television after the news: politics, pop groups, personality parades, soaps and cooking. He fell asleep in the chair.

Mary looked across at him and sighed.

On Saturday he weeded the garden and cut the lawn; on Sunday, Mary prepared a picnic lunch and they spent the late morning on the moors. However the weather broke unexpectedly and following several rolls of thunder and some lightning, it rained vertical stair-rods. They arrived back home at one o'clock, missing the worst of the weather and in time to watch a John Wayne cowboy film on television, then 'Songs of Praise,' followed by 'Last of the Summer Wine.' As the theme music increased in volume and the credits rolled up over the bucolic scene, Angel's mobile phone rang out. He was surprised at the interruption: it could only be police business and he knew it must be urgent. His pulse increased and his heart began to bang in his chest, as he reached down into his trouser pocket and yanked the phone out.

'Angel,' he said expectantly.

'Sorry to bother you, sir. This is PC Donohue. We have been called out to a vehicle fire on some farmland in Skiptonthorpe. It is a big, black Mercedes saloon. We attended and when I reported it in, the desk sergeant said you had it on orders that you had to be advised on this number of any sighting of this vehicle.'

'Yes. Yes,' Angel said excitedly. 'That's right. Tell me, what's happened?'

'We had a treble nine call to a vehicle fire by the back road behind Summerskill's farm on the top side in Skiptonthorpe. We attended promptly, so did the fire service.'

Angel's knuckles tightened. 'Don't tell me the fire service have been crawling all over the site?'

'Yes, sir.'

He wrinkled his nose. 'What's the state of the fire now, lad?'

'It's out, sir. The fire service are just damping down.'

'Right. When it's safe, get them off the site, mark it out and treat it as a crime scene. And stay there. I'll be with you in about fifteen minutes.'

'You'll need your wellies, sir.'

CHAPTER FOURTEEN

Angel soon found the country road behind the farm at Skiptonthorpe. He saw the police car with two policemen inside at the side of the road. He drove up and parked behind it.

And he certainly did need his wellies. The rain had now ceased but it had been a very heavy downpour.

He clocked the gap between some bushes where the Mercedes had been driven ten yards off the road onto the edge of a ploughed field, dumped and ignited. A lager can, several newspapers and magazines had been dumped close by and were now drenched and part trodden into the mud.

There was a smell of burning rubber and petrol.

He could see that the car's rear window and windscreen had been smashed, most of the upholstery and carpeting burned out, and all the internal surfaces and controls were black, but the metal parts, the wheels and the tyres were intact.

He squelched precariously at a careful distance of about twenty feet from the car looking down at the sodden earth.

Two policemen came up to him wearing high-visibility yellow coats and flat hats.

'Good evening, sir. Good evening, sir.'

Angel looked up from the muddy field, his lips tightened back against his teeth. 'Look at all those footprints. You've had a bigger crowd here than there was at Reggie Kray's funeral!'

The two policeman exchanged glances but said nothing.

'I want you to mark out this area with DO NOT CROSS LINE tape, at a minimum of fifteen feet from the car and this break in the bushes. I want to preserve every track in the mud from around the car and up to the road.'

'Right, sir.'

'When you've done that, I shall want some illumination. It'll be dark in a few hours. I expect to be here all night. I shall want one of you to go to the stores and get a lighting kit and generator.'

They dashed off and opened the boot of their car.

Angel dug his hand into his pocket, pulled out his mobile and tapped in a number. 'Is that the National Crime and Operations Faculty? I want to call on your specialist to advise on motor vehicle tracks, please. It's very urgent.'

It was 2100 hours and the section of the field and the break in the bushes had been marked out with DO NOT CROSS tape attached to stakes in the ground. The road was full of activity and thronged with police vehicles. Angel had requested more uniform to secure the site and manage the few interested members of the public occasionally rubbernecking as they passed. SOCO had arrived and also an HGV with low loader to transport the car away. Angel was with a DI Ince and a photographer from the NCOF who were working on pads on their knees making plaster casts and taking measurements with a steel tape.

It was going to be a busy night.

'Two coffees, Ahmed. Smartish.'

'Right, sir,' he said and went out of the office.

Angel looked up Gawber, rubbed his scratchy chin, sniffed and said, 'They've ditched the only lead we had, Ron.

We had the number, colour and make of their car. Now I have no idea where they are and we have absolutely nothing to go on!'

'You brought the NCOF in, sir?'

'Aye. I'm clutching at straws, Ron. I'm hoping they can, maybe, save the day by reading something from the tyre tracks. There were some pretty sharp outlines in the mud.'

'Yes. And they've turned nothing up?'

Angel's miserable face told him that they had not. 'It's early days.'

'Has SOCO brought the Merc back here, sir?'

'No. It's been taken to Wetherby. I wanted the boys in the lab to go over it. They might turn up something. There's also a lager can and some papers and magazines that were littering up the scene. They might help. Don Taylor's working on them now.'

Ahmed came in with two beakers on a tin tray. They reached out and helped themselves.

'Ta, lad,' Angel said. 'Now, nip down to SOCO and ask DS Taylor if he's anywhere with that lager can and those papers I brought in.'

Ahmed nodded and went out.

The phone rang. Angel picked up the receiver. It was Harker.

'There's something in the post. I want you up here,' he growled. There was a loud click and the line went dead.

Angel pulled a face as if he needed a tooth pulling. He turned to Gawber. 'It's the super. I've got to go.'

He trudged up the corridor and knocked on the door.

'Come in,' Harker bawled. He was sitting at his desk, head down reading.

Angel closed the door.

Eventually Harker looked up, stared at him, blinked, scratched his head and said, 'You look a right mess. I thought it was Bill Oddie dressed up for a funeral.'

'I have been up all night, sir. I haven't been home yet.'

'Yes. I heard. It was only a car fire, wasn't it? Did they really need you there to turn the hose on,' he said sarcastically.

'It's the Glazer gang's Mercedes,' Angel replied strongly. 'They've obviously changed over vehicles there. I am trying to find out what they've changed to, and where they are now.'

'I know. I know, but it's nowt to do with you, lad. I haven't authorized it. It's not your case.'

'It might be, sir. Could be Glazer, or one of his gang, who murdered Harry Harrison.'

'I thought that *that* was down to Spencer.'

Angel licked his lips. 'It *could* still be him. I'm waiting for some forensic from SOCO. That should settle it.'

Harker sniffed.

'Come on, lad, admit it,' he said expansively. 'Admit it. You're in the dark, aren't you? You're just fishing. Harrison was well known among the crooked fraternity. It could be anyone of a thousand villains who might have heard of the big money he'd got hold off.'

'No, sir. I'm *not* fishing,' Angel replied resolutely. 'There's a reasonable bet it's Glazer or Spencer.'

Harker shook his small, grotesque, gargoyle-like, misshapen head.

'Well, press on with it, then. Time is money. I know you have a personal reason for trying to get Eddie Glazer back behind bars. I know he gave your pride a proper singeing, but don't let that cloud your judgement,' he said waving a sheet of paper he was holding. 'But I didn't call you in to talk about your pride. It's about this.'

'What is it,' Angel said, holding out his hand.

Harker didn't pass it to him. 'It's a bill from a Mrs Reid for damage to a door and door jamb, lifting of floorboards, scratching of paintwork … it goes on. Four hundred pounds. *Four hundred pounds*! It's hardly a legitimate charge against this department. Who's going to pay for *that*?'

'That would be damage the Glazers did, searching Harrison's flat. It would be down to *them*!'

'Can't charge it to them,' Harker snapped. 'They're not here. We don't know where they are. You just said so. You let them get away. They just slipped through your fingers.'

Angel's eyes flashed. 'They were heavily armed.'

'So were you.'

'You *know* the situation, it made attack on our part impossible. It would have been against standing orders. There could have been a bloodbath.'

'I only know what you tell me in your reports, which I know are sometimes heavily edited.'

Angel's jaw tightened. He pursed his lips. He breathed in and out a couple of times. This argument was going nowhere; he refused to let Harker wind him up any further. 'If you don't want me for anything else, sir, I'd like to go home and get tidied up.'

'Yes. You'd better. Got to maintain standards.'

Angel turned to go. He opened the door.

'What about this four hundred pounds?' Harker fumed, his face as red as a judge's robe. 'I can't put an expense through like *that*. It's down to you, you know.'

Angel sighed.

'Why don't you knock it off the two million I found under the floorboards, sir?' he said and he closed the door.

Ahmed saw the imposing figure whiz past the window panel in the CID office door. He caught up with him and followed him into his office. He was carrying two EVIDENCE envelopes and an A4 paper file.

'What've you got, lad?' Angel boomed.

'From DI Taylor, sir. He found a fingerprint on the lager can; it's of a prisoner on the run, Eric Oxenhope, otherwise known as "Ox".'

Angel's eyebrows shot up. He took the file, opened it and began reading it aloud. '28 years of age. Last known address 266 Gosforth Road, Whitley Bay; 12 previous convictions for … oh … erm … yes.' His voice dropped as his interest waned. He turned to the next page in the file and read: ' "Oxenhope's prints were also all over newspaper. Also one other first finger and thumb from right hand of person unknown, thought to be female. Put on file. Handwritten number in pen in margin of page 2, might be helpful." ' Angel dropped the file grabbed the thinner EVIDENCE envelope, opened it and pulled out a well-thumbed, dried out newspaper in a cloud of aluminium powder. He turned to page 2. Sure enough in the margin was a six digit number. It was written in large handwriting with a blue felt pen.

' "603670", Ahmed. Does that number mean anything to you?'

'No, sir. Is it a phone number?'

'It could be. Find out what it is, lad. I'm going home. Be back in an hour or so. Ring me if anything urgent comes in.'

It was 10.22 a.m.

After a shower, a shave, a clean shirt, two cups of tea and two slices of fresh toast and butter, Angel was as pleased with life as a man guilty of murder, being awarded an ASBO.

He got in his car and returned to the station.

As he opened the office door, the sun was shining in through the window. The shadow formed a hopscotch pattern on the parquet floor. The room smelled of microwaved dust and fingerprint ink. He realized how hot it was. He opened the window and part closed the Venetian blinds. He took off his jacket and put it on a coat-hanger on the side of the stationery cupboard.

The phone rang. He leaned over the desk and picked up the receiver. It was Taylor. He sounded pleased about something.

'I have examined the clothes and personal effects of Simon Spencer, sir, and have taken various specimens and examined them, but found nothing to link him with Harry Harrison.'

Angel was deflated.

'Oh?' he said, wrinkling his nose. 'Right, Don.'

'But I *have* found tiny spots of blood on both the left and right shoes of a pair of trainers taken from the farmhouse,' he added brightly. 'And I have managed to isolate a sample of the blood and can confirm that it is from the dead man, Harry Harrison. I don't know who the owner of the shoes is, but they are size 10, and they were found at the right hand side of the hearth in the kitchen.'

Angel's face brightened. 'Ah. Right, Don. Thank you. So that definitely puts Spencer out of the frame. The murderer of Harrison is the owner of that pair of trainers.'

'That's it, sir, exactly, and my money's on Eddie Glazer.'

Angel smiled, thanked him again and replaced the phone. He rubbed his chin a moment and then picked up the phone and tapped in a number.

Ahmed answered.

'Is DS Gawber there?

'No, sir.'

'Put a call out for him, and then come on in here.'

'Right, sir.'

A minute later a smiling Ahmed came into Angel's office. 'I must have missed you coming in, sir. I think I have found an answer to that number.'

'Right, lad. Good. What is it?'

'The telephone company say that that number is almost certainly a Bromersley subscriber because it doesn't fit any other exchange in South Yorkshire.'

'Right, Ahmed,' he said. 'Well done. Now go to the officer on the front desk and ask for a charge sheet for a Simon Spencer at present in Bromersley General and address unknown. The charge is fraud. I might find a few other charges to add onto it, but that'll do to hold him, when the hospital discharges him.'

Ahmed made for the door.

'And see if you can find Ron Gawber on your travels,' he added as he reached out for the phone.

'Right, sir.' The door closed.

Angel tapped in 9 for a dialling tone for an outside line, then 141 so that the station number wouldn't be given out, then the six-digit number. He sat back in the chair and rubbed his chin. He had no idea who might be answering. He had no idea whom he was calling, but he had been through this exercise a thousand times in this business.

The phone was soon answered. A pleasant-sounding woman's voice said, 'Webster's Holiday Caravans. Can I help you.'

Angel frowned. 'Can I speak to Harry, please?' he said.

There was a short pause and then she said hesitantly, 'Did you say Harry?'

'Yes, please.'

He licked his lips as he wondered what she was thinking.

There was another pause.

'I think you must have got the wrong number. There's nobody here of that name, now, sir.'

Angel smiled: he wasn't a bit surprised.

'We did have a Harry Shaw working for us, but he left two years ago,' she added.

'No. That wasn't the name,' Angel said. 'But anyway, I *was* thinking about a caravan holiday,' he lied.

'You need to speak to our Mr Webster. He's busy with a customer. Can I get him to call you back?'

'Is that Graham Webster?'

'No. It's Mortimer, actually.'

'Oh? Mortimer Webster, of course. No. I'll ring back later on today. Or I might call in. What's the exact address again, Miss?'

'Goat Peg Lane, off Kingsway. We are at the end. You'll see a lot of caravans on your right hand side. Sheltered on three sides with trees. It's a lovely site. You can't miss us.'

'Right. Thank you. Goodbye.'

He replaced the phone slowly and thoughtfully.

There was a knock at the door. It was Gawber.

'Come in, Ron. Right on cue.'

He updated him. He told him about the number in the newspaper and said that the gang might be connected with Webster's caravans.

'But it may have nothing to do with it, sir. That number might be the combination number of a railway station security locker, or some other locker, or a bank account, or just about anything.'

Angel wasn't pleased. He knew that what Gawber had said was perfectly valid. But he was desperate. Clutching at straws.

'Just because it was obvious, doesn't make it wrong.'

'No, sir,' Gawber said. 'Of course not.'

Angel stood up and reached for his jacket. 'Well, it's a lovely sunny day. Do you fancy looking over a caravan? We could take afternoon tea out in the country.'

Gawber frowned. This wasn't the Angel he knew.

Angel drove the BMW along Kingsway and down the narrow, twisted track called Goat Peg Lane. The lane was in need of resurfacing, so he had to approach slowly. They soon passed a neat and simple sign that read: 'Webster's Caravans.'

'Been down here before, sir?' Gawber said.

'No. I hope we can turn round at the end. Don't relish reversing back all this way.'

The lane twisted and turned and eventually opened out revealing a long, white-painted, breeze-block building with a big sign announcing that they had arrived at a three-star caravan site big enough for 120 caravans and that it was owned by a Mortimer Webster. Beyond it, they could see trees, which appeared on three sides and sheltered an area where there were forty pitched towing caravans. Spaces for more caravans led away, as far as the eye could see. There were a dozen or so motor-caravans grouped together at the back. Some of the towing caravans had small canvas tents erected around their doorways, while some had cars parked next to them and people enjoying the sun in deckchairs or sunbathing on the grass. All the vehicles were in neat rows, facing south. In spaces where there were no caravans, small weather-protected posts in the ground with sockets for electricity to be supplied to the vans could be seen standing in the manicured turf. In addition, there were several cars and caravans travelling slowly on the service roads between the pitches. They were clearly arriving, or leaving the site for other pastures.

Summer was in full swing in Bromersley.

A sign said, 'All visitors please report to reception.'

The sound of an internal combustion engine driving a lawnmower spoiled the quiet of the summer's day.

Angel didn't drive through the entrance. He stopped the car behind the long building and switched off the engine. Gawber and Angel got out of the car, walked through the open gate, stepped up onto a veranda and through the low doorway into the reception office.

A young woman was sitting at a desk behind a high counter. She pushed back her chair and came up to greet them.

'Good afternoon, gentlemen. Can I help you?'

Angel gave her a smile. 'We want to see Mr Webster, miss, if you please.'

The insistent drone of the lawnmower engine became louder as it came closer to the office.

'Mr Webster is cutting the grass. But I think he's coming in now.'

The engine died.

'Yes, he is,' she said. 'Please wait here. He won't be a moment.'

She returned to her desk.

Angel nodded and said, 'Thank you, miss.'

Seconds later, a middle-aged man in khaki shorts, hat and T-shirt came in to the office. He was wiping his forehead with a handkerchief. He looked at the two policemen and said, 'Are you waiting to see me?'

'Mr Webster?'

'Mortimer Webster at your service, gentlemen,' he said loudly. 'Sorry if you've had to wait. Got to keep the damned turf down. A bit of rain and a bit of sun and it grows like fury this time of the year, you know.'

Angel winced. He put up a hand and wagged his first finger at him to invite him to come closer; when he did, Angel leaned over the counter and whispered, 'I'd like to talk to you on a matter of great confidentiality. Can we go somewhere quiet?'

Webster's eyebrows shot up. He looked round like a nervous kitten. 'Oh yes.'

Angel frowned. He put his first finger vertically across his lips, from his septum to his chin. Then he took out his wallet and showed it to Webster, who read it carefully, nodded then without a word pointed to a door. They went through the door into a small room that served as an office.

'We are looking for a gang of crooks. At least two of them are on the run from prison, and one of them is wanted for murder.'

Webster looked shocked. 'This is a respectable site, Inspector. I don't accept any riff-raff.'

'I am sure you don't intend to, but a caravan site might prove to be a good hiding place for them. I'd like to take a look round the site and see if I can see them without them recognizing me first.'

'Of course, you must. But how are you going to manage that, Inspector?'

Angel rubbed his chin. There was a problem.

Ten minutes later, having removed his tie and jacket, opened his shirt collar and turned up his suit trousers, Angel donned Webster's big khaki hat and sunglasses, climbed onto the high seat of the lawnmower and began driving it up and down the grass pitches of the caravan site.

Gawber returned to the car and waited patiently, keeping the entrance under observation in case Glazer's mob moved on or off the site.

Angel spent forty minutes on top of the mower, cutting the grass, traversing the site so that he could see every single vehicle without arousing suspicion. He worked his way up to the far end of the site where Webster had an area allocated for extra-large caravans or RVs, Recreational Vehicles, as Americans called them.

And there they were. The Glazer gang – all five of them – next to a big American chromium-plated monster.

Angel's pulse raced. He had to steady his shaking hands on the mower's handlebar. He drove as close to them as he could. They hardly spared him a glance. Eddie, Tony and Kenny were seated on deckchairs at a round table with a big red umbrella over it. Eddie was reading a newspaper. Tony and Kenny were chatting. Oona Glazer was stretched out nearby on a towel on the grass sunbathing, while Kenny was sitting on the motor-caravan step, smoking a cigarette. Within arm's length of each of them was a wine holder with a bottle of Bollinger nestled in it.

Angel turned the mower round and pointed it at Webster's office. He had a chill in his heart and determination in his belly.

CHAPTER FIFTEEN

It was 4 p.m., Monday, 23 July. It was three hours since Angel had discovered the whereabouts of the Glazer gang and, in that time, not a minute had been wasted.

The sun continued to beat down and it was still very hot.

Through binoculars from the veranda of the site office, Angel observed that the Glazer gang was now pulling out chairs and hovering round the table outside their RV. They appeared to be gathering to eat a meal. That was the sign he had been waiting for. He was planning to drive an unmarked 4 x 4 car, towing a touring caravan along a service road slowly towards them, while, at the same time, another 4 x 4 and caravan, was to be driven by Crisp in his shirt sleeves and open-necked shirt, along a different but parallel service road in the same direction. The two cars and vans were to look like two unrelated family caravans moving to pitches to park and set up for the night.

The moment had arrived. Angel got in the cab of the 4 x 4 and started up the engine. He waved Crisp on and they moved off driving at 10 mph along parallel service roads towards the Glazer gang. It wasn't far. The journey would take only thirty seconds or so.

Many caravanners were in deckchairs or on towels on the grass applying suncream in the still hot sun. Two young girls in swim suits played a simple ball game with rackets across an unoccupied caravan pitch. Angel was concerned for their safety: this was always the worry when trying to arrest an armed gang in a public place.

The slow, short journey was tense but uneventful. When they were about twenty feet away from Glazer's RV, both 4 x 4's stopped as planned. Eight police in riot gear piled out of each caravan at speed, their Heckler and Koch G36C assault rifles drawn and cocked. At the same time, from a loud speaker perched on the roof of Angel's vehicle, his loud, distorted, commanding voice could be heard.

'Eddie Glazer, this is the police,' he said commandingly. 'You are under arrest. So are your friends. Lie down on the grass, immediately. *All* of you.'

The Glazer gang looked up from their meal, stunned. They saw the sixteen rifles aimed at them, dropped their cutlery and, wide-eyed, looked across at each other.

People sunning themselves nearby heard and saw what was happening. Some of them bustled their children and their families inside their vans for safety. Some others stood up and gaped at the scene curious or astounded.

The police closed further in on the gang and screamed, 'Get down. Get down. Get down. Hands on your head. Hands on your head.'

There was a sudden move from Glazer's brother, Tony. From a kneeling position, he reached out to a pocket in his coat draped around the chair where he had been sitting.

'Leave it,' a policeman yelled and a warning shot was fired at the chair. A bullet ricocheted from the chair and made a loud metallic click.

Tony Glazer pulled back his hand. 'All right,' he screamed, holding up his hands from a kneeling position. 'All right. I give up. I give up.'

Everybody on the caravan site heard the rifle shot. More sun-worshippers dived into their caravans or cars for shelter.

'Get down,' a policeman yelled at the Glazers.

'Get down. Get down,' the call was repeated interminably by the police.

The five members of the gang lay close together prostrate on the grass. The police closed in still directing their rifles at them. Two of the policemen dragged the chairs, with coats hanging on them, wine stand, boxes of wine, Oona's handbag and the loaded table hastily towards the caravan and away from their prisoners.

On cue, a big black police van rocked quickly along the grass through the caravan site towards them.

Angel arrived at his office the following morning at 8.28 a.m. He was as bright as the Chief Constable's MBE, and ready to supply the necessary evidence to the prosecuting barrister of the Crown Prosecution Service. This man, a Mr Twelvetrees, would use Angel's information to obtain a remand order at the magistrates' court next door later on that morning for each of the five members of the Glazer gang.

There was a knock at the door. It was Gawber.

'I've checked the shoe size of each of the men, sir. The only size 10 is Eddie Glazer.'

He wrinkled his nose. 'No possibility of an error, Ron?'

Gawber shook his head. 'The others are 11s and 12s, sir.'

Angel nodded thoughtfully. 'That confirms it then,' he said firmly. 'Eddie Glazer's barrister will have to work damned hard to get him out of *that*.' Then he added grimly, 'Glazer will die in prison.'

'I'll push off and check they'll be ready for court,' Gawber said.

He went out as Dr Mac had arrived at the door.

'Can I come in?'

Angel smiled.

'Ah Mac, you're always welcome here. Come on in.'

The Scotsman closed the door. Angel pointed to the chair by his desk. 'Sit down. It's very early for you, isn't it, Mac? Worried some tealeaf might have nicked your porridge?'

'None of your lip, laddie,' Mac said maintaining a dour face.

Angel grinned.

Mac leaned across the desk and said: 'I suppose you'd like to hear the result of the DNA comparison between the loose hair found on the body of Alicia Prophet, which SOCO confirmed belonged to Charles Prophet, and the flesh content in the saliva of Carl Gaston's mouth, taken from that handkerchief of yours, wouldn't you?'

Angel paid Dr Mac very serious attention. 'It certainly has a bearing on a case I'm working on, Mac,' he said expectantly.

'Well, I can tell you quite positively, that there are enough similarities to prove that Charles Prophet *was* indeed the biological father of Carl Gaston.'

Angel raised his head.

'Thank you very much indeed, Mac,' he said, nodding slowly.

That was the very last piece in the puzzle and Angel felt a warm, comfortable feeling in his chest. An excited shiver ran up and down his arms and hands. He now knew exactly where to find the mysterious Lady Cora Blessington. He considered the position a moment; there was still a lot to do before he could make the arrest.

After exchanging the usual courtesies, Dr Mac left.

Angel rushed down to the CPS office and discussed and determined with Mr Twelvetrees, prosecuting barrister, the charges to be made against the Glazers. They were duly typed up and presented to their solicitors before attending the court. Later that morning, he had the satisfaction of seeing the five of them whisked away on remand in a Group 4 van.

The rest of the morning and afternoon, he spent a thoughtful and busy few hours making his plans. He briefed Gawber and then went home for a shower and an early tea.

At 5.25 p.m., Angel left home and drove the BMW to the end of Victoria Crescent, a side street in Bromersley. He parked it in such a position that he could see down Victoria Road; the road comprised Georgian stone-built houses which had been converted over the past century or so to offices mostly occupied by solicitors, accountants, estate agents and building societies. He particularly wanted to clock all the comings and goings from the offices and small private car park of Prophet and Sellman. He looked at his watch. It was 5.32 p.m. He did not expect that he would have to wait long.

At 5.35 p.m. Charles Prophet strode confidently out of the big blue door, crossed the car park to his car and drove away in the direction of The Feathers Hotel on Market Street. Seconds later the elegant figure of Karen Kennedy appeared on the front step. She looked round, turned back, put a key in the door lock, turned it, withdrew it, stuffed it into her swish Gucci handbag and strode swiftly the few paces across the car park to her white Mercedes. Seconds later, she drove away from Angel with a roar of the engine and turned in the opposite direction towards Jubilee Park on the other side of town, where she lived in a new block of flats on the main Doncaster Road.

Angel started up his BMW and followed her. She lived less than two miles from the office and she had, on good days, been known to walk the short distance. Today she was driving her white Mercedes competently through the side streets of Bromersley, skirting the busy shopping areas and eventually turning onto Doncaster Road. Angel kept a discreet distance behind her until she reached her block of flats. She pulled up on the main road, switched off the ignition, got out of the car and made her way towards the main door of the flats.

Angel followed her and was slowing his car, when, at the last moment, he touched the accelerator and the BMW jerked forward which caused his front bumper to hit the rear of the beautiful Mercedes making an unpleasant, expensive crashing noise.

Karen Kennedy heard it. She looked back angrily, took in the situation and stormed back down the path towards him.

Angel frowned and bit his bottom lip. He reversed the BMW back a few feet from the Mercedes, stopped the car and got out.

Karen Kennedy stood on the pavement edge, hands on hips and surveyed the damage. Then she stared at Angel and said: 'Oh, it's you. I might have known it. A stupid policeman! Haven't you any brakes on that car?' All the charm so well controlled at the office of Prophet and Sellman had completely disappeared.

Angel said: 'I am very sorry, but you did stop rather abruptly and without any signal.'

Karen Kennedy's face went scarlet. 'There was no need for a signal,' she stormed. 'My brake lights would tell you I was stopping. Anyway, I had locked the car and was ten feet away, when you crashed into it!'

'I didn't know you were going to stop and park here on a main road,' he said calmly. 'And I don't think your brake lights were working.'

'They were working perfectly well yesterday when the car was returned after a service.'

'And look how far you are from the kerb. A traffic policeman would book you for being more than ten inches from the kerb. It's not safe for other traffic.'

She looked down at the distance the wheel of the Mercedes was away from the kerb. 'That's all right,' she said. 'Must be only five or six inches, that's all.'

Angel looked shocked. He shook his head. 'Be reasonable. It's at least eighteen inches, Miss Kennedy … far too far … if this matter was taken to court, you'd have a job to prove the actual distance.'

She looked up at the sky and fumed: 'Huh! Give me strength. Wait there, Inspector Angel,' she said determinedly. 'Wait there. I won't be two minutes.'

'I'm not going anywhere,' Angel said evenly. 'I'm not leaving here until I have details of your insurance company.'

She stormed off through the main door into the flats. When she was out of sight, Angel turned away from the door, dived into his pocket and pulled out his mobile.

He tapped in a number. The phone was promptly answered.

'In position, sir,' Gawber said. 'We can be there in a minute.'

'Right,' Angel said. 'When I send you a text, come in fast.'

'Right, sir.'

'Out.'

Angel cancelled the call and set up his phone to send the letters 'OK' to Gawber by text and held it in his pocket ready.

A moment or two later, Karen Kennedy appeared through the door. She had discarded her handbag and was bearing down on Angel with a small camera. Her face was grimly set, determined to win the argument.

Angel pressed the button on the phone in his pocket and sent the text.

Karen Kennedy stormed up to him waving the camera.

'This will settle all argument, once and for all, Inspector. Don't think that because you're a policeman that you're above the law.'

'I don't,' he replied. 'I just don't think that you have any idea about driving a car.'

Her beautiful eyes glared at him. 'I have passed the advanced driving test and I have the certificate to prove it,' she said confidently. 'Please move out of the way. Let me take a photograph of this. My car is very properly parked and no more than six inches from the kerb. Eighteen inches indeed, huh!'

Angel stood back to allow her access with the camera.

She photographed the two cars from various angles and was busy lining up a shot of the damage to her car resulting from the crash when a Panda car pulled up quietly behind Angel's. Gawber, SOCO's Taylor and WPC Leisha Baverstock got out and came up to Angel.

Karen Kennedy was intent on taking the photographs and didn't seem to notice them at first, then she suddenly spotted the uniform on the WPC.

'What's this?' she said, her eyes darting from one to the other and then back to Angel. 'Called for reinforcements, have you?' She waved the camera at him. 'It won't do you any good, Inspector. The camera doesn't lie.'

DS Taylor looked at Angel who nodded for him to proceed.

The policeman took out his warrant card, showed it to her and said, 'I am Detective Sergeant Taylor. Is that your camera, Miss?'

'Of course it is,' she snapped.

'Do you own any other?'

'No. Why?'

He held out his hand. 'Will you give it to me, please?'

'No,' she said. 'Certainly not. This is evidence. Your inspector is not going to get away with *this*.'

'I am a forensic officer and I need to examine it, in connection with the murder of Alicia Prophet.'

Her jaw dropped. 'Alicia Prophet?'

The colour drained from her face. She stared at him, then at Angel. She swallowed and said, 'But I have nothing to do with that. It has nothing to do with me.'

Taylor stood there with his hand held out.

'May I have the camera please?'

Karen Kennedy handed him the camera.

WPC Baverstock stepped forward and got hold of her by her elbow. 'Come along with me, miss.'

Angel returned to the station in his car with Gawber, WPC Baverstock and Karen Kennedy, while Taylor rushed off with the camera in the Panda car.

At the station, Angel told Karen Kennedy that he would be inviting her to make a statement under caution, and suggested that she contacted her solicitor. He then left her in an interview room in the competent hands of WPC Baverstock and made his way up the green corridor with Gawber to his own office.

Gawber closed the door and they both sat down.

'Whatever made you suspect that it was Charles Prophet dressing up as Lady Blessington then, sir?' Gawber said.

Angel breathed in deeply, sighed and said, 'The very first thing was that curious photograph of his wife, Alicia and Lady Blessington cosily having tea together on the patio. It was, I expect, taken shortly before the murder, only hours or days, and placed casually among the other photos to help try to establish the authenticity of Lady B. Prophet said it had been taken about six months earlier. If it had been, it would have been in January, and it would have been almost certainly too cold for tea in summer clothes outside on the patio, with flowers, trees and shrubs, rich in foliage, and some rose bushes and other flowers in full bloom. So I knew that it was a lie. I began to wonder why he needed to lie about a trivial thing like that. I got to thinking that he was about the same height as Lady B. Once I went down that lane, I was well on the way to solving the riddle. The fact that Prophet's wife was blind made me realize that she never knew what he was dressed in or what he looked like. I was puzzled when he said that *he* had taken the photograph. Obviously, I knew I had to check that out closely. If it was another lie, then it indicated that he must have had an accomplice. There was no camera in the Prophets' home. I checked with SOCO. And there were no other recent photographs anywhere in the house. They were not a family that habitually took photographs as some families do. So I had to widen the search. Karen Kennedy was the first obvious suspect. I had to get possession of her camera without raising her suspicions, hence the contrived accident with her Mercedes. I thought she'd be just the sort of person who would *have* to win a dispute. Photographs were the obvious proof, and if she had a camera, she'd *have* to use it.'

Gawber looked up at him in amazement.

'Fantastic. But why did he spread the scene with orange peel. That didn't fit the illusion of a titled lady committing the murder?'

'That was done by Margaret Gaston. She came on the scene via the back door, shortly after Prophet had committed the murder and departed by the front door. She had brought some shopping requested by Alicia. Saw the dead woman, shot in the head, assumed, correctly, as it happens, that it was Prophet, and because she would have done anything for him – after all, he was the father of her child – thought she could assist him by fogging the issue by dispensing orange peel around the body, just as if the murder had been committed by Reynard. She'd no doubt been reading all the gory details about that multiple murderer in the papers. She had some oranges in the shopping. Then she thought she must dispose of the rest of the oranges to remove the source, so she put them in the dustbin.'

'And the shopping in the pantry and the change on the draining board were also left by Margaret?' Gawber said.

Angel nodded.

The phone rang.

It was Taylor.

'Got it, sir,' he said triumphantly.

'It *is* the same camera?'

'Yes, sir. There are similarities on the prints in three places. A bit of fogging on the top right hand corner and two identical places where the film was scratched as it was rolled on to the next exposure. That's more than enough to be absolutely positive it's the same camera.'

'Right,' Angel said and replaced the phone. He turned to Gawber. 'Come on. It's just about sewn up.'

Angel switched on the recording machine, gabbled off the time and date and those present, looked across the table at the woman and said: 'Miss Kennedy, you said that on the day that Alicia Prophet was shot, Mr Charles Prophet was in his office the entire afternoon.'

'Yes,' Karen Kennedy mumbled.

'Please speak up, for the benefit of the tape,' Gawber said.

She looked at her solicitor, who nodded encouragingly.

'Yes, I believe I did,' she said.

'Well, we now know that that is not true,' Angel said. 'Would you like to … revise your evidence?'

She glanced at her solicitor, who nodded.

'Yes. Yes. I suppose I must,' she said slowly. 'After lunch … he was not in his office all afternoon. At about twenty minutes to two, he went out.'

There was a long pause.

Angel looked across the table at her. She looked back at him.

'You know exactly what happened,' Angel said, 'because you and he planned it together, didn't you?'

She didn't say anything.

'If you plead guilty and tell me what happened, it will reduce your sentence, Miss Kennedy. Those are the rules.'

Her solicitor nodded. She licked her lips.

'Mmmm,' she began. 'Well, he took a suitcase of clothes and stuff and drove his car to Wells Street Baths and parked it in the public car park. He bought a ticket and took the suitcase into the baths. He changed into the blue dress, wig and stuff in a cubicle there and … he deposited the suitcase with his ordinary clothes in a locker. He came out of the baths and took a taxi to his own home. Walked into the house. Set the world straight with Alicia. Got her to sit on the settee. And, as he told me afterwards, shot her in the head. He said that she wouldn't feel a thing or even know it was going to happen. Then he reversed his steps, took the taxi back to the baths, changed and returned to the office by car.'

'What happened to the blue dress, the wig and other clothes?'

'Late that same night, he brought them to my flat and we burned them in the incinerator in the boiler house in the basement.'

'And why did he choose such old-fashioned clothes?'

'Don't know. Said he'd seen a picture of a woman in a blue dress somewhere. He modelled himself on that. He said he preferred the long dress because it would conceal his legs, which he thought might be a giveaway. He said the picture didn't show the woman's feet. He was glad of that because, I couldn't find any women's shoes large enough to fit him.'

'You were aware of his intention to murder his wife?'

She swallowed, looked down at the parquet floor then nodded.

Gawber said: 'For the purposes of the tape, Miss Kennedy nodded.'

'Do you know *why*?' Angel said.

'He was bored with his wife,' she said timidly. 'He said that she was blind and a drag on him, and that he wanted me. He'd inherit her money, and he said he'd never be found out. He said that you, the police, would naturally suspect him, but if I stuck by the alibi they wouldn't find out. The plan was to establish a non-existent person, have her murder his wife virtually in front of three eye-witnesses, then make her disappear. He said it was the perfect crime.'

Angel raised his head. 'What was that?' he said. He wrinkled his nose and shook his head. 'Don't you know yet, there's no such thing as the perfect crime?'

She burst into tears.

He turned to Gawber and said: 'I've heard enough, Ron. Bring him in and charge him with murder.'

THE END

OTHER BOOKS BY ROGER SILVERWOOD

YORKSHIRE MURDER MYSTERIES

Book 1: THE MISSING NURSE
Book 2: THE MISSING WIFE
Book 3: THE MAN IN THE PINK SUIT
Book 4: THE MORALS OF A MURDERER
Book 5: THE AUCTION MURDERS
Book 6: THE MISSING KILLER
Book 7: THE UMBRELLA MURDERS
Book 8: THE MISSING MILLIONAIRE
Book 9: THE MISSING THIEF
Book 10: FIND THE LADY

Please join our mailing list for free Kindle crime thriller, detective, mystery, romance books and new releases!

www.joffebooks.com

Follow us on Facebook, Twitter and Instagram

@joffebooks

Thank you for reading this book. If you enjoyed it please leave feedback on Amazon, and if there is anything we missed or you have a question about then please get in touch. The author and publishing team appreciate your feedback and time reading this book.

We're very grateful to eagle-eyed readers who take the time to contact us. Please send any errors you find to corrections@joffebooks.com

Printed in Great Britain
by Amazon

76324021R00106